A tree is felled to make ~~a~~ motorway — and a ~~shrine~~ is Dresus, King of the ~~?~~ kingdom and now plots a terrible revenge...

Patti and Simon have had a difficult time explaining away their fourteen years absence from the earth (their *Touchstone* adventure). The scientists still question them, convinced they are not telling everything they know.

One night, as they are watching television, Ezon appears on the screen. The children of the East have been kidnapped by the wizards of Cromsutti Morthern, the swordmaker, has decreed that they must help in the search for them.

To fight the magic powers of the wizards, Ezon enlists Moorgate and Atholle, who is sent to the mysterious island of the Ancients where he meets the Subservients and gets a map. Gadua, the sailmaker, provides a compass, and the boy Charbonne introduces them to the sinister Corvey — skeletons with green eyes who ride phantom horses, and come and go through the dream world.

Peter Regan creates a magnificent tapestry full of colour and mystery, through which is woven the sinister thread that represents Nadair, most powerful and evil of all the wizards in Cromsutti...

Another great adventure for Patti and Simon in the world of the Four Kingdoms.

PETER REGAN

Revenge of the Wizards

Illustrated by

Pamela Leonard

THE CHILDREN'S PRESS

To Sarah

First published 1991 by
The Children's Press
45 Palmerston Road, Dublin 6

ISBN 0 947962 61 1

Typeset by Computertype Limited
Printed by Billing & Sons

This book is financially assisted by
The Arts Council/An Chomhairle Ealaíon, Ireland

Contents

PART THREE

EPILOGUE

PART ONE

1. The Withered Tree

Patti Ahearne and Simon Morgan lived in Oakten.

Although a town, Oakten was a green and pleasant place, with trees, mainly oaks, dotting the streets. It had a picture-postcard prettiness about it, especially in winter when the snow lay on the spiky hedgerows and bent the evergreens into podgy floppiness.

Patti and Simon were best friends. She was almost twelve; he was almost eleven. Officially, they were much older. You see, they had been missing for fifteen years on a secret magical adventure, and had not grown any older. When they returned all their friends were amazed to see they were still children instead of young adults. This created many problems for Patti and Simon. Their old friends were fifteen years older. Some were married and had children. They had turned into different people, so Patti and Simon had to find new play pals the same age as themselves. That too was strange, as they were now in the same class as children who had not even been born when they were last at school.

In Patti's case, even her family had changed. Before the adventure she had neither brother nor sister; now she had a sister aged thirteen, who was two classes above her at school and never stopped lecturing her. When Simon saw the problems Patti was having he was glad he was still the only child in his family.

It had all taken a lot of getting used to!

Because of Patti and Simon's mysterious age 'freeze', articles were sometimes published about them in the papers and they were still interviewed from time to time on television. Every so often they were brought away on week-ends to a place where scientists attempted to probe the mystery that surrounded them. But Patti and Simon always pleaded loss of memory regarding the magical world they had visited. Normally they did not tell lies, but this was a special white lie — just one; the only one they could remember having told in all their lives. To absolve their consciences they kept their fingers crossed. They just had to; they had been warned not to mention the world they had been to — the world of the Four Kingdoms. There had been evil in that other world and it could follow them and do harm. Theirs was not just a secret; it was a matter of life and death.

Although all this was a great strain on Patti and Simon, they coped very well. Simon still went to Patti's house and occasionally Patti would go to Simon's, and they both rallied one another's morale as good friends always do.

Sometimes they would go down the fields and sit and stare at the withered tree and the lip of the rock quarry under which they had found the stone that had been responsible for the great adventure of which they had been part. But sadly, the quarry and the fields surrounding it were under threat. Two years after their return, a colossal motorway had been planned and the surveyors were already marking the rolling fields and the brambly patches of bushes for the lie of the concrete roadway. The children feared for the quarry and the withered tree, feeling that these were the only objects left to remind them of the wonderful enchanted world they had entered. That was not quite true. There were other objects; the crown and the sword which the children had found at the foot of the withered tree and hidden in their homes; and the two rings that they had been given in that enchanted world and which they always wore. Sometimes the rings glowed a red spiral of misty light, but nobody knew this except the children. Nor did anyone else realise that the rings had the power to whisk them back to the world of the Four Kingdoms.

Although the children did not know it, the withered tree held a dark secret. There was someone trapped inside it — someone from the other world! The children usually spent a lot of time thinking about that other world. When they did, they thought of two people in particular. One was Ezon, their friend and protector during the great odyssey of their adventure. The other was Moorgate, a wood-elf who had used woodland magic to conjure the powers that had turned a sworn enemy, Dresus, the King of the West, into the withered tree above the quarry.

Work began on the new motorway. The rumbling earth-moving machines excavating the foundations moved through the green countryside and soon reached the quarry. As it stood in the path of the motorway, it was decided to remove the tree. A workman was detailed to saw off the trunk and dig out the stump with a pick-axe. But he felt nervous about destroying the tree — he was superstitious and believed that bad luck would result if it was interfered with — so he decided to leave the job until the next morning and see if his boss could be persuaded not to remove the tree.

That night the tree swayed, then it shuddered. Its roots whipped out of the ground, the bark broke from the branches and the trunk — and a man slipped from the peeling of the tree. He put his hand to his side, then to his forehead. Once he had a crown and a sword but now they were gone. Gradually a sense of realization swept over him and he stepped stiffly from the shallow tangle of roots and walked past the roadworks. The dark shadows of the machines and the flashing hazard lights frightened him. He had no idea where he was, but inwardly he was in a state of seething rage. All he could think of was Ezon and Moorgate and how much he wanted to kill them. He grunted and raved and shook his fist at the dark sky. He walked until he came to the main road where cars sped past. He cowered back into the darkness and kept away from the road. Coming across an old hut, the shabby door half off its hinges, he crept in and hid. Eventually he fell into a troubled sleep, a nightmare mingling of past and present.

Thus did Dresus, one-time king — now no longer a king —
spend his first night.

Hunger forced him out the following night — and it was
marvellous how quickly it sharpened his senses! He stole some
clothes from a line in a garden and discarded his old outsized
mediaeval-type garments. He was no longer afraid. He set out
again along the road, keeping to the side and clenching his
fist at the traffic. He was hungry and furious. Furious that
he had to walk such long distances. Furious that he had to
go hungry. When he got to Oakten he did not quite know
what he should do next. Even the street lights were a puzzle.
He went into a public park and sat down on a convenient
bench, where he was soon overcome by sleep.

When he woke it was daylight and he went back into the
town. The shops were open. In a supermarket he stole some
food, returning to the park to eat it. Later he re-entered the
supermarket and picked up a purse with money in it. But
it was not easy to work out the value of the money. He decided
it was easier to steal than to reckon prices. But he knew he
would have to re-educate himself if ever he was to get on
in this strange new world. So in the evenings he went into
the pubs and sat listening to the customers discussing various
subjects, most of which he did not understand. He learned
a lot from watching TV in the public bar.

Gradually his natural cunning reasserted itself. After three
months he gave up stealing. He bought a smart suit, rented
a large yard with office space, changed his name to Norman
McCoy and sold second-hand cars. He cheated his customers
and it made him feel so good that at times it seemed that
he had forgotten all about wanting revenge on Ezon and
Moorgate. But he never quite forgot. Yet he was happy in
this new world of worlds, and he was to stay happy until
something catastrophic happened — and then it was too late
to do anything about it. But that was all in the future, and
nobody knew the future, not even Dresus.

2. The Children Disappear

The land in which Ezon lived was called the Kingdom of the East. There were three other kingdoms in Ezon's world: the Kingdom of the West, Cromsutti in the north, and Hasutti in the south. All four kingdoms were separated from one another by a massive ocean called the Great Ocean.

Ezon, with the glory of former feats behind him, was much renowned in the City, where the King and Queen of the East, Azor and Matoi, lived in the peaceful splendour of the Royal Palace. With them also lived their two children, Toria and Panri, who had been part of Patti's and Simon's great adventure, and who were identical in looks and age to the two earth children. They had once been held captive in the West by Dresus and Patti and Simon had helped to rescue them. Of course Ezon had been the real hero, and Moorgate too.

And there had been the two fantastic flying horses which belonged to the royal children and which were kept in the royal stables. Patti and Simon had ridden them high above the clouds and across the Great Ocean to the West and deep into the snowy wastes of Hasutti. Ezon's father, Ozez, who had been a powerful wizard, had put a special spell on the horses, and only Toria and Panri or their look-alikes, Patti and Simon, could ride them. And that was the main reason why the children had been brought to the Four Kingdoms. When the royal Prince and Princess were held captive in Dresus's island prison, they were the only two people who could ride the horses and so travel, with Ezon, the great vastness of the Four Kingdoms to rescue the captives.

All that was in the past. As of now, Ezon was married to Meridia, once a maiden in the shrine of the Ancients. They lived in the house formerly owned by Ezon's father, who had been slain by the wizards of the West. Ezon lived quietly with

Meridia, meticulous in his role as Commander of the Army of the East, and sometimes consorting with his friend Fraiter who was a master of disguise and intrigue. He did not like going into his father's magical shrine. It made him feel uneasy, and it worried him that Meridia spent so much time there. Here Ozez's parchments, wands and other ceremonial emblems lay, only feet away from the marble altar and powerful magical circle where once the evil wizards of the West had shackled Ezon and cursed him with the green hue which had blemished his body for so many years during his youth, and was only later removed in the shrine of the Ancients by Meridia's priestesses.

One day Meridia asked Ezon to go into the shrine with her.
    'I don't wish to. I want nothing of wizardry,' he retorted.
    'But you are Ozez's son. His whole life is in there.'
    'I remember my father from the table where he ate, not from the altar of demons.'
    'But he only did good.'
    'That did not prevent him from being murdered.'
    But Meridia coaxed and coaxed until she persuaded Ezon to enter the shrine. The first thing he saw was the stone — the green-speckled white rock which Patti and Simon had found in the quarry and which had brought them to Ezon's world; when they returned to earth it had magically been restored to the Kingdom of the East. Now it rested on a marble column.
    Meridia walked up the seven steps which led to the top of the column. She reached out and held a crucible of water over the stone. The stone glowed. Steam began to rise from the crucible. Then it burst into a cold flame before tapering into a circular shimmer. Then a voice was heard. It was the voice of Morthern — Morthern who lived beneath the ice-caps of Hasutti, deep in the bowels of the earth, and who used the earth's gases and entrapped flames as mighty furnaces to fashion weapons, one of which was the sword Ezon used

(and still had) to slay dragons, decimate armies and repel all sorts of perils. The voice boomed out with an authoritative ring: 'I have heard that the wizards of Cromsutti are seeking retribution for the demise of Dresus and the disappearance of the wizards of the West. Ezon, Moorgate and the two children Patti and Simon are under threat. The wizards of Cromsutti are bent on a terrible revenge, for they know that the wizards of the West are doomed in the mountain caves to which the magic of Moorgate banished them. No intercession can free them — unless Moorgate is destroyed. You have been warned. I will do all I can to help. . . .'

Morthern had spoken and the ring of flame from the crucible subsided. Meridia placed her hands on the stone and closed her eyes. She seemed to fall into a trance, and as the stone glowed she levitated off the ground. She raised her hands and pointed towards the black dome above. A dark shape passed over her and she opened her lips, speaking in a rasping voice, 'Ezon, your time will come, as will the elf's. Our host is eleven. And of that host I am superior to the others.'

Ezon was startled. The voice had been that of a man, but it was not that of Morthern. It had an evil ring to it. The dark shape left Meridia and she floated down on to the steps. Ezon felt a great surge of resolve sweep over him. He rushed over and took her from the shrine, into the shelter of his arms. Outside she came out of her trance and Ezon vowed to steel himself against whatever evil was afoot.

For a few months all was well in the Kingdom of the East, but then children began to disappear. Not small babies nor toddlers, but children between the ages of ten and eleven. Children whose eyes were full of happiness and who smiled with impish innocence. Children who turned houses of stone into living homes. Children whose play lit up the day, as the sun or wonderfully coloured landscape of flowers and balmy meadows could not.

The children disappeared at night, after they had snuggled warmly and fallen asleep in their beds. Nobody ever saw them vanish, or heard their footsteps on the stairs or on the bare wooden floors. Nobody ever heard the windows or the doors open as the children were taken, never to be seen again. Nobody saw or heard anything.

As each day passed more children disappeared. Parents were heartbroken. Even though they stayed up all night and stood on guard over their sleeping children they would still disappear and the parents would be none the wiser as to how it happened. Not only were they heartbroken; the children who were left became terrified of whatever dark presence was snatching their brothers and sisters in the middle of the night. They lost the urge to laugh and play. The City became a dull, lifeless place.

Finally, Azor, the King, commanded Ezon and Fraiter to solve the dreadful mystery. They journeyed the land on horseback, sometimes being gone for weeks, searching villages, towns, even the mountains and the far off plains. But they could not find even a clue, much less the whereabouts of the children. Sea-coves and harbours were visited in the hope that someone might know if children were being shipped to some distant forsaken port. But still the mystery was unresolved and there was absolutely no inkling of what had happened to the children.

Ironically, after many false trails Ezon and Fraiter were called to a house only a few yards from the Royal Palace. They were conducted upstairs and shown an empty bed where, only the previous night, a child had slept. Both parents were overcome with grief. Their child was missing. Beside the bed a tangle of cobwebs was draped over a press, the top of which was covered in dust. A name was scrawled in the dust, and it seemed to sway under the veil of cobwebs. Ezon looked at the name and at that instant everything concerning the missing children seemed to fit into place. But he said nothing to Fraiter, not until they got outside the house. The name in the dust read

'Nadair', whom Ezon knew to be the most powerful and evil wizard in all of Cromsutti. He now understood the reference in the shrine to the number eleven, and one of that number being greater than the rest. There was an alliance between Nadair and ten other wizards of Cromsutti. What was more, Ezon felt certain the missing children were in Cromsutti, imprisoned by the wizards. The evil voice in the shrine had probably been Nadair's!

When Ezon got home he told Meridia.

'Don't go,' she said. 'It is only a trap.'

Ezon shook his head. 'It is in the stone and of it. And if only for the children's sake, I have to help.'

Meridia knew Ezon was right. There was only one course of action open to him. He would have to make the long journey to Cromsutti on his own, without Fraiter, as he did not want his friend to be put under the threat of the evil wizards' magic.

Ezon went to the Royal Palace and was immediately ushered into the presence of the King and Queen. He told them about hearing the voices of Morthern and Nadair in the shrine, of finding Nadair's name scrawled in the dust, and his fears that the missing children had been taken to Cromsutti. The King and Queen immediately ordered him to go there and search for the children, and if necessary, confront Nadair. Ezon's past record as a warrior capable of succeeding in the most dangerous of adventures was beyond doubt. He was the one person most likely to succeed in such a mission, and the King and Queen felt fully confident in their choice. Also, it was good to know that Morthern was on his side.

As he bade Ezon farewell, the King said gravely, "Nadair may not stop until he has taken every child — regardless of age — from the Kingdom. In doing so the Kingdom would be drained of its life-blood. There would be no future ... no hope ... and our Kingdom would eventually become a barren, enfeebled place which would face almost certain ruin."

Ezon understood the significance of the King's words.

Shortly afterwards he left the Palace, passing the palace guards, the outer floral palisades, and the fringe of the cobbled stable yards where he knew the Prince and Princess, Toria and Panri would be tending their horses. Their hearts must have been heavy too, for if they disappeared, in years to come there would be nobody left to rule the Kingdom, and there would be no subjects to rule over. In the words of the King, the Kingdom would become a desolate domain, empty of people and life.

Ezon knew what he had to do — go to Cromsutti, find the missing children, and confront Nadair and his host of vile wizards.

3. Strange Happenings in Oakten

Once a month Patti and Simon were brought to a red-bricked building where the scientists had their laboratories. On their next visit, a month after the withered tree disappeared from the quarry, they lay down, as usual, on stretcher-like tables. Metal bands were placed upon their heads. A mesh of wire connected the bands with monitors. Codes and words kept coming up on the screens. Eventually, they went blank, and turned green in colour. The scientists mumbled in disappointment. Nothing of significance had been discovered in *that* experiment.

Patti and Simon sat up, still with the wires connected to their headbands. Just then, as Simon glanced at the monitors, the screens flickered momentarily and an image appeared on them. It was Ezon, dressed in warrior's clothes. But just as quickly as the picture had flashed on, it faded from the screens.

'Do you know who that was?'

'No,' replied Simon.

'It wasn't Robin Hood, was it?' Patti felt smart with this retort, but really she was as nervous as a kitten.

One of the scientists became irritated. 'What do you think

we're running here, cable television?'

Luckily they left it at that. There were no more questions. They undid the tangle of wires and gave the children appointment cards for their next visit. It was like going to the dentist, only worse — much worse. You see, they were always afraid that they might inadvertently betray their secret.

Two nights later strange bumping noises were heard in Patti's home. The family could hear heavy thuds and the sound of furniture being dragged across the floor. Terrified, they waited until the noise ceased; then when they went into the room from which it had come, they saw that everything had been moved. Chairs were lying on their sides. The table was upside down. The carpet was rolled up. The parents rang the scientists who brought monitors and equipment, but nothing registered. Not until the very end of the night — and then the sound on the monitors went crazy with evil laughter.

Patti heard the laughter, and told Simon about it next day.

'That laughing comes from the Four Kingdoms,' she said, grim-faced.

Simon believed her. Luckily, the bumping noises and evil laughter were never heard again. Perhaps the beings who caused it thought that one warning was enough.

4. Enchantments

Moorgate, the wood-elf, sat sharing a thoughtful pipeful of tobacco with the pitiful person beside him: Atholle. A surge of sea waves broke strongly on the rocks below them. The day was cold and the leaves lay in a clogged mass on the island's forest floor. After the great adventure to rescue the royal children Moorgate had been brought to the island at his own request, on a ship belonging to Azor, King of the East. He lived on the island with Atholle, an acutely absent-minded person who wore his clothes as they should not be worn. Atholle was almost completely useless but he had magic food pouches to eat from and a wine pouch to drink from. They never emptied and were always full of succulent cooked food, and thirst-quenching wine. Atholle lived in a tree-house and Moorgate had to do the same, as too many wild animals prowled the island — especially at night — and the only safe place was in the trees.

Atholle was full of chat. He was busy retelling the story of the enchanted stream full of fish which once were living people, and of Santander, who had succeeded the evil tyrant Dresus as King of the West, and had, not so long ago, been a fish in that stream. Moorgate had heard of Santander and how Dresus had tricked him and thrown him on to the green sward beside the stream where he turned into a fish.

Atholle also mentioned a magical glade, and when they were finished smoking the pipe he took Moorgate to see it.

'This glade is special. If you walk through it you become a duck, then a rabbit, even a golden chalice, Watch!'

He walked jauntily into the glade. A puff of yellow smoke broke about him. When the smoke lifted he was gone. In his place appeared a duck. Another puff of smoke erupted and the duck changed into a rabbit. The rabbit twitched its whiskers and hopped along the glade. The yellow smoke puffed again and the rabbit was lost in the cloudy fuzz. When the smoke lifted the rabbit was gone, and a gold chalice stood upright on the rough grass.

'Is that you. Atholle?' queried Moorgate. 'Can you hear me?'

'Yes. I can't move! I can't walk! How am I to get out of the glade? Am I a chalice?'

'I'm afraid so.'

'What an end to my life! If it rains I will fill to the top and overflow! Or I will be smothered by leaves and never be seen again. I could even become rusty!'

'Gold doesn't rust. You are made of gold.'

'Worse still! I am valuable. Some rogue will steal me.'

'That won't happen. Nothing will happen.'

'Tragedy! Tragedy! Tragedy!

'Why a chalice?' thought Moorgate to himself. 'Something that can't move. Really, Atholle is *very* silly!' Before he had time to reply yellow puffs of smoke broke out all over the glade. They burst in quick succession and when the smoke cleared, the glade was full of gold chalices, just like the one Atholle had become. Voices spoke from the chalices, all pleading for help. All the pleas mixed with one another until all sense of identity was lost. The quake of voices had an upsetting effect on Moorgate. He almost wished the wind would rise and toss the glade's heavy boughs with rippled lashings of leaves and so drown out the cries of anguish.

Just then the voices stopped, and the glade became silent. Moorgate shouted out Atholle's name. Atholle did not reply immediately, but when he did Moorgate told him to keep on talking — at least until he, Moorgate, could find a rock to throw into the glade to mark the spot where he was located. That way he would know exactly which of the gold chalices held Atholle prisoner.

'You won't hit me with the rock?'

'I won't.'

'What then?'

'I will come back tomorrow and try to rescue you.'

'But I can't be rescued!'

'I can read forest leaves. There may be a message to tell how you can be rescued.'

'It is autumn, the leaves will all be withered. I am doomed!'

Moorgate realized there was a lot of truth in what Atholle had said. Sadly, most leaves would be dry and shrivelled, whatever information they might contain obliterated by the autumn decay. He found a rock and threw it close to the chalice in which Atholle was imprisoned. The voices began to speak again. He would have liked to have stayed a little longer, but he knew that his words of comfort would only have been drowned by the drone from the chalices. Anyway, it was getting dark; the sun had begun to set. He would come back in the morning.

Next day, he returned to the glade in a very down-hearted mood. Each leaf he had examined was badly withered and whatever message it might have contained was indecipherable. The glade was silent, as if a deep sleep had overcome the captive occupants. Moorgate had to shout several times before Atholle answered. When he did, his first question was, 'Did you find any leaves that weren't withered?'

Regretfully, Moorgate had to answer No.

'Well, I dreamt of a place where there are leaves — lovely fresh green ones.'

'Dreams are not reality.'

'No, they are better. Reality is too horrible. ... See what it has done for me. ... Turned me into a chalice!'

'Tell me your dream.'

'Go to the enchanted stream. There's an oak-tree. Keep to the left of it. Walk and walk and walk, until you come to a hill, then another, and another. There you will see a pond. You can have a rest. A deer will pass by. Follow it. It will bring you to where the leaves are always green.'

Moorgate did as Atholle instructed. When he came to the pond he halted. Nothing could be seen except the still water of the pond and the rising slope of a hill. He waited for an hour, and then, almost out of thin air, a heavily antlered deer stood beside the pond. What happened next was something Moorgate would never forget. The deer moved up over the hill and crossed the top, where it turned into a wolf. Moorgate felt a strong desire to run away. His terror could not have been any greater if the wolf were to change into a bear. By the time they reached the top of the next hill that was exactly what happened. To his horror the wolf changed into a huge black bear that stood upright and snorted the air angrily. The

bear waited for Moorgate to approach, but the elf kept his
distance. The bear then walked ahead, going down on all fours,
its furry back arched in a lazy curve as it went up what was
to be the last hill.

On the brow of the hill the bear turned into a man. He
was enormous; fat and flabby. Black pouch-like circles drooped
beneath his eyes. The man pointed over the rough hill-top
ground to four trees crowned with lush green leaves. Moorgate
went to the trees and the man followed him. Moorgate wanted
the man to speak, but he remained silent. Instead, he pointed
at one tree in particular and walked away.

Moorgate muttered timidly after him, 'I can't get up into
the tree!' And in truth, he could not; he was too small.

The man came back and lifted Moorgate into the tree.
Moorgate sensed immediately that the changeling was totally
evil. He could feel it in his touch. He was half afraid he would
be grabbed by the throat and strangled, but the man did nothing
except help him to grasp a branch and shove him up into
the cluster of branches. Then he left and walked back down
the hill. Moorgate was to see him again but not for weeks,
and that, to a wood-elf, was a very long time indeed.

Moorgate had leaves to read. But the task was not as easy
as it might seem. Certain messages could be read by day; but
not those connected with spells and matters of a magical nature.
That information became visible only by the light of the moon.
So he had no choice but to sit in the tree until darkness fell
and the strength of the night showed the moon's face in the
sky.

As twilight faded the stars began to show overhead. The
moon shone brightly. Moorgate smiled, it was a perfect night.
He climbed busily about the tree, plucking leaves and examining
them for a likely message. Some leaves were blank, and others
had messages that were of no relevance. He stuck doggedly
to the task. His eyes became strained and his arms ached as
he hung on to the branches. At times he felt like lying down

and going to sleep, but he kept on searching until he had almost the whole tree stripped of leaves, and only then did he find the information which had eluded him. It formed in fine silver writing and told of a tree on the far side of the island, which jutted out on a rocky promontory into the sea. The tree had berries and Moorgate was to bring a handful to the glade and place all except two in the chalice that held Atholle. Of the two remaining berries he was to keep one and give the other to Atholle, so that both would be able to leave the glade without mishap. His work done, he found a hollow nook in the tree and fell asleep.

He did not sleep for long. When he awoke he found hot tongues of flame flickering about the tree. They shot up all around Moorgate and he expected the tree to be on fire, but it wasn't. The flames crushed together. Then there was a deafening roll of thunder and a jagged flash of lightning split open the sky and shot down into the flames. The ground quaked and Moorgate held on to the tree for dear life. He sensed that at any moment he would be tossed into the whirling vortex of orange flame and white lightning. But the flames dwindled and died out. The tree stopped quaking. Moorgate felt a sudden flow of wind blow against his face. It seemed to have a faint whispering moan. Then he nearly leapt out of his skin. He could hear a voice which gradually became louder and more distinct. He relaxed his hold on the tree and sat down to hear what the voice had to say:

'Little man, there is a plot afoot to lure you and Ezon, the son of Ozez, into a trap. The wizards of Cromsutti, under the leadership of Nadair, have reason to seek revenge for what you did to Dresus and the wizards of the West. As for Ezon, revenge is sought for the part he played in the overthrow of Dresus. Already you have witnessed the guile of Nadair. It was he who lifted you into the tree and led you to find the leaves.'

Moorgate was not excessively worried at the mention of

Nadair's name. It had been easy for him to conjure up the devastating magic which had once imprisoned the wizards of the West in boulder-sealed caves. If Nadair threatened him he would make similar response.

'Who are you?' asked Moorgate.

'I am not one to answer questions. What I offer is advice.'

'I would like to be able to see you.'

'That would be impossible. I am nowhere near you. I am not even on your infernal island. If you must know — I am Morthern. And believe me I have better things to be doing than wasting my breath explaining my identity to an elf.'

Moorgate was taken aback. Morthern lived thousands of miles away in Hasutti and yet he was speaking to Moorgate as clearly and loudly as if they were sitting next to one another.

'I'm sorry,' apologized Moorgate. 'I have been through a lot. I can't help but feel suspicious.'

'Perhaps there is a lot I should explain. But time will unfold the complexities. The wizards are plotting your downfall. Better go along with it, whether knowingly or unwittingly; free Atholle from the glade and leave the island. That is what the wizards want, just as they want Ezon to go to Cromsutti in search of the children who have been stolen in the East. There they will crush him.'

'But I can't leave the island. There is no way of getting off.'

'You can build a boat.'

'I don't know how.'

'Cleverness has ways around obstacles. There will be no problem. You are clever and a good carpenter. Take Atholle with you. Tell him I said so. Tell him to leave the Dial hanging from the tree the berries are on.'

'What Dial?'

'He has not shown it to you?'

'No.'

'That is his purpose on the island — to give the Dial to

travellers who want to seek me out. The Dial directs travellers to me. Tell Atholle to leave it in the tree. It will be there when he gets back. When you leave the island the wizards expect you to go to Cromsutti. Go there, and eventually you will meet Ezon. The wizards can only wreak their revenge in Cromsutti as that is where their magic is most powerful. Go there, and rebuke their evil vengeance.'

'A boat would never get to Cromsutti from here.'

'Absurd! Of course it would. Atholle has the food pouches. And you will have my guidance on the journey. One important matter: You are to stop off at the island where the Ancients live.'

Moorgate's heart skipped a beat. The Ancients were regarded as gods and no living person had ever set eyes on them.

'But that island has no air,' he said. 'We would suffocate. Anyway, we wouldn't be able to find the island.'

'Humbug! You will find it, and Atholle will set foot there. That nuisance does not need air. He can breathe without it. He knows so little about himself. Not even that vital and obvious detail. Do you remember the children, Patti and Simon?'

Morthern need not have asked. Of course Moorgate remembered Patti and Simon.

'The Ancients have consented for them to be brought to Cromsutti.'

'But those children have no real powers.'

'Maybe not, but they are involved with you and Ezon, and until the wizards are done away with, their involvement along with yours (and the two royal children to a lesser extent) will be needed to witness the final demise of Nadair and so add potency to the removal of the curse.'

'What curse?'

'The curse the wizards have unleashed by kidnapping children from the East. It is also believed that Patti and Simon's presence is needed here in the Four Kingdoms to break the power of the curse. And remember, Atholle has to go to the

Ancients to seek advice on how best the wizards can be brought
to heel and their evil sorcery destroyed. There will be other
lesser reasons which will only become apparent later.

'For now, free Atholle from the glade and build a boat and
set sail for the Ancients before going on to Cromsutti. I will
use whatever powers I can to prevent the wizards from finding
out you have been to the Ancients. The wizards have already
used their evil influence to free Dresus from the shackles your
magic put him under.'

'You mean, he is free of the tree?'

'Yes, but do not worry He is where the wizards cannot bring
him back. The Ancients would have to consent to it. And
they will, but only when the power of the wizards has been
broken. But first things first. Free Atholle from the glade.
Safe speed, and good luck!'

Morthern's voice flagged, and Moorgate realized that his
contact with the great man was gone. A shudder of excitement
surged through him. He knew he was on the verge of a
tremendous odyssey. He was delighted, and all his past anxieties
evaporated. He felt like singing a song, but instead he curled
up in the tree and watched the stars until he fell asleep. It
was a happier-than-happy sleep. It was great to be suddenly
at ease, and not to have to sleep with one eye open.

Next morning he found the tree, took the berries and freed
Atholle from the glade.

Atholle was in a sulky mood. 'You certainly took your time,'
he growled. 'I thought you were never coming back.'

Moorgate ignored him. He took a bamboo from the
undergrowth and some bark from a tree. When they got home,
he opened the chest he had brought to the island on board
Azor's ship. He took out his carpenter's tools and laid them
to one side for the construction of a boat. Then he returned
to the bamboo and bark. He hollowed the bamboo until he
was sure it would make a satisfactory blow-pipe. Then he
ground the bark to a powder and heated it until it became

bubbly and sticky. He already had arrowheads and shafts which, to all appearances, looked like darts. He dipped the darts in the bubbling powder and placed them on a slab to cool. When the drying process was finished he wrapped the darts in a strip of cloth.

Atholle, still sulking, was not at all interested in what Moorgate was doing. Even when Moorgate mentioned that he had been talking to Morthern and that they were to go on a great adventure in a boat, the news did not seem to have much appeal. He treated Morthern's name with indifference. But the idea of a boat pleased him, especially if it were to have a white sail, and two big oars for him to row with. Moorgate could have little ones — they would have to be small on account of his size.

Anyway, when they got back to the tree-home Atholle was starving and he ate and ate from the magic food pouches. And when he was finished eating he was restored to good humour and could not thank Moorgate enough for rescuing him from the glade. Only when Moorgate started saying elf-prayers over the blow-pipe and darts did he hush. He had never heard anybody say prayers before, and he was very moved. He would have liked to say a few prayers too, but he did not know anybody to pray to; there was no way he would pray to Morthern because, years ago, Morthern had left him all alone on the island. As for the Ancients ... well, like everything else he just did not know ...

5. Shipwreck

The ship which carried Ezon north ploughed through the heavy heave of the open sea. The crew scowled uneasily as sheets of spray burst over the bulwark. The deck tackle was wet and slippery, and the creak of the spars strained in the following wind. Below, in one of the cabins, Ezon and the ship's captain sat at an oak table studying maps of Cromsutti's ports and inland towns.

Cromsutti was a fabled land, as rich in gold and diamonds as it was scarred by volcanoes, with mountain caves that sheltered fabulous treasures and fiery dragons. It was a land of contrasts. It was flat; it was mountainous. It had vineyards, orchards and diligently tilled fields; it had barren deserts. It had brooding red volcanoes and snowy mountain peaks. There were dragons, herds of flying horses, and mountain lions which never slept. And some said there were goblins and water-demons. Cromsutti was not really one kingdom, but a series of domains ruled over by chieftains and local warriors.

But there were also wonders of a much more gentle nature than dragons and volcanoes. There were waterfalls which cascaded perfume. Rings, necklaces and bangles came from deep in the ground through wellshafts. Ships laden with satins and silks called to port once a year and gave away merchandise to any girl who came by. But there were also sad things; people who lived as slaves, who toiled night and day, year in, year out. And there were women who had their children taken from them, and who never saw them again. Ezon had shuddered at the thought. It was because of missing children that he was now voyaging through the rough ocean to Cromsutti.

The crew were wary of Ezon, especially his sword; they had seen it drawn from its scabbard and the glint which shone off the blade showed it was no ordinary weapon. Some said they saw fire flicker in the blade. What was more, the crew had heard of the feats executed by the sword, and knew that it had been given to Ezon by Morthern, the forger of the most powerful of weapons. It was well known that it was a dragon-slayer and could absorb dragon-flame and fire. To add to their fears, Ezon seemed prepared for trouble. Not only had he the sword, but he wore warrior-clothes and had a quiver full of arrows and a bow, as well as the long spear with which he was so adept.

The sailors were quite glad that Ezon stayed below deck most of the time, but on the second-last day of what was to be an ill-fated voyage, something happened which made the crew even more wary of having him on board. A gigantic bird rested in the shrouds. Ezon was called for and flighted arrow after arrow at the bird's cowled form. But they all floundered and fell back on to the deck. Only when Ezon drew Morthern's sword from its scabbard did the bird loosen its taloned grip on the shrouds and fly off over the Great Ocean, its loathsome shape lost in the vastness of the sky. But as it soared out from the shrouds a cluster of red berries fell to the deck and a gold chalice sprouted from where the burst berries lay. One of the crew tried to grab the chalice but it seemed to melt and left a burn mark on his hand. He grimaced in pain, and had to be led away for treatment.

The rest of the crew watched in silence. During the night-watch, they spoke in whispers and later they went to the Captain and said they had had enough of Ezon, and that when the ship anchored in Cromsutti they wanted him to take a different ship back to the East, or else they would mutiny. Not too reluctantly, the captain agreed.

But the ship never reached the safety of harbour. During the night the wind had risen to storm force and when, at dawn, the first greyness of the morning light showed on the face of the sea, with its mountainous wind-whipped waves, the crew knew they were at the mercy of the elements. Ezon suspected the storm was caused by Nadair and his fellow wizards.

All tackle was made secure and the ship's wheel lashed with heavy ropes. The hatches were closed, and not a man was allowed above deck. They all waited in the cabins, sombre and repentful, as the pounding and jarring repercussions of the waves swirled and tossed the ship in splintered pain. The buffeting was so severe that the Captain ordered the cabin-lights dowsed, for fear they would smash and torch the ship in flame. And in the darkness the ship burst open and torrents of water plunged into the cabins, the ship's galley, the hold. The ship's great oaken beams were ripped asunder. Some of the crew perished in the cabins as at last the ship sank. Others, Ezon among them, were hurled out into the angry depths, through holed gashes in the ship's side.

Unlike the others, Ezon did not lose consciousness immediately. His bow and spear had disappeared in the deluge of water, but the sword in its scabbard was still securely buckled to his back. The weight of it almost kept him under and he was on the verge of discarding it, but he willed himself to swim to the surface where he managed to hold on to some loose debris. He had gone down with the ship but he had risen from its watery grave. How he survived the storm, unconscious but instinctively clinging to a splintered beam of the ship's oak, he would never know. But survive he did, and when he woke he was far from the sea. He was in a rocky place of stone and hills. There was a river in the distance and a glowing red hillock.

Unknown to Ezon he had been rescued from the perils of the storm through the intercession of Morthern with the Ancients. He had lain in a weakened stupor for days on a remote beach. Then, when he awoke, it was as if he were in a trance. It was something akin to sleep-walking. He tramped through forests, over mountains, and crossed wide river-courses. He passed cascading waterfalls which parted and showed jewelled walls with windows and doors, and the happy shining faces of the water people who lived inside the clefts. He walked, zombie-like, past small dumpty men and women who were of snow and lived in the high mountains; people whose worse fate in life was to avalanche down the mountain slopes, and to have to suffer the indignity of plodding back up to the snow-line, before the strong valley sunlight took the plumpness from their arms and legs.

There were places where night never fell; and places where there always was night — where stars continuously plumed thin trails across the sky. There were silver stars, red stars and yellow stars. Stars that waned and waxed — becoming larger and smaller, smaller and larger. Skies that had three suns, and skies that had three moons. Castles which one day were there and the next day were gone. There was always something new and magical.

There were many, so many wonderful extravaganzas on Ezon's twilight journey, but he remembered none of them.

Ezon did not fully awaken until he came to a rocky plateau beside which a small hillock radiated a sinister red glow. Gradually a circle of red hot lava seeped through the ground and he was not able to move out of it.

6. Morthern's Warming

Patti and Simon had been brought by her father to keep the appointment with the scientists. Her sister Claire came too. She did not like Simon, and Simon knew it, he stuck out his tongue at her. That made Patti laugh, but, looking at her sister's furious face, she knew she would have to try very hard to be nice to Claire, and she hoped Simon would do the same. Maybe Claire would try, too, and one day very soon they would all be good friends and there would be no more bickering.

At the sprawling building which was the scientists' research centre, the children were brought into a changing-room where they put on the usual orange-hued pyjama-like suits. A lady in a white coat led them down the maze of corridors.

'If she gives you a pill to swallow, don't take it,' whispered Patti.

'Why not?'

'It'll be drugged to make us talk. I think they suspect we saw something last time and didn't tell.'

'But if they make us swallow it?'

'Say you're sick. That you'll vomit.'

The lady brought them through a door that swung inwards, into an enormous hall which was really a laboratory. There were lots of scientists in white coats with identity cards on the lapels, rows of computers, and a balcony with radio receivers and transmitters.

'I was right,' thought Patti. 'This is a much more elaborate set-up than usual. They know we're concealing something!'

Patti and Simon lay down and the lady harnessed wires to their foreheads and the back of their heads; the wires led into a big computer beside them. Nearby was a screen, not as big as the screen in a cinema, but much bigger than any of the computers. They were left lying on the stretcher-like tables while the scientists mumbled and played around with the computers and all the other gadgetry. As they looked up at the domed roof, an opening appeared and a huge radio telescope was lifted up on a hydraulic platform until it pointed at the open sky. By now all the scientists were busy. Some were up on the balcony. Others supervised the computers. A few took notes and gave instructions. Then two of the computers blew fuses, and those manning the radio receivers complained of static.

Unknown to everyone, the rings that Patti and Simon wore began to glow. The volume of static lowered to a bleep, and a voice could be heard on the big screen. It boomed out, 'Be warned, evil forces are afoot! Beware of those wizards who seek revenge — the wizards of Cromsutti!'

It was the voice of Morthern!

A computer caught fire, and the lady in the white coat quickly disconnected the pad of wires from the children. She saw the rings on their fingers glow, but when she looked again the glow was gone. Someone dowsed the smoke-ravaged computer. The children got off the tables and waited for the interrogation to begin.

But the scientists said nothing. They did not ask questions.

After all those unproductive sessions, at last they had something tangible — they had Morthern's voice on tape. But all their efforts to assess this nugget of reality failed.

Nor could the computers or telescope help them. They watched and listened to the galaxies; to whole planets and stars and rings of orbiting debris throughout the furthest reaches of space. And when nothing was found, only then did they turn their attention full-time on poor Patti and Simon.

From now on, their every move would be watched.

7. Red for Danger

Moorgate's boat sailed smoothly through the balmy placidness of the Great Ocean. He steered the rudder, while Atholle watched the sail billow. The latter, his magic food pouches gathered about him, was worried about leaving the Dial unattended on the island. He was afraid Morthern would punish him. Occasionally he began to whimper and Moorgate had to remind him that they had left the island on Morthern's instruction, and not to fret.

After two weeks at sea Atholle became so bored he was willing to try anything for a change, even jumping overboard and swimming in the Great Ocean. He leapt over the side in his clothes. He had never been in the sea before; in fact, he had never even swum before. It made him feel vigorous and carefree. He threw all his clothes back into the boat. First the jacket which he wore as a trousers of sorts; then the trousers which he used as a jacket. Then his shirt. Then his shoes; they were too heavy and inclined to drag his feet down as he swam. His mind was now in less of a muddle, and for the first time in his life he fully understood the craziness of wearing his clothes the way he did. Although the boat sailed along quickly he was able to swim effortlessly alongside as the bow cut through the waves. He did not want to get back into the boat. He felt clever in the sea. In the boat he would only be awkward and ridiculous again.

Moorgate looked down at Atholle. His eyes shone brightly in admiration. Atholle was a fine swimmer, and the little elf was glad for him.

Then Atholle jerked his head under his body and, like a cormorant, he flipped beneath the waves. He stayed under water for almost ten minutes, and Moorgate became worried. When he resurfaced it was only to flip back down again and swim to the deepest depths of the Great Ocean. Memories which he had forgotten flooded the recesses of his mind. He remembered living with Morthern in Hasutti, and — even more vividly — Morthern bringing him to the island and leaving him the magic food pouches and the compass-like Dial to direct travellers to the icy world of Hasutti and Morthern's underground forges. He could remember it all as clearly as if it had happened yesterday. But now he remembered something more; something that had been hidden from him until now — his life before Morthern. He could remember, but he could not understand. For a second something inside him seemed to say: 'Atholle, you are of the Ancients. Alone we stand, and alone you will exist.' He felt a tinge of sadness at the words, though he did not quite understand what they meant.

Atholle was so overcome by the sheer marvel of being able to swim that he locked out everything except the wonder of the underwater world which lay before him. The deeper he went, the duller and more obscure the depths became. But he could make out the shape of what looked like mountain peaks rising from the floor of the Great Ocean. Below the peaks it got darker, until he could see nothing at all except a white powdered dust. Just as he was about to turn and break back to the surface, a bright light shining from one of the underwater peaks attracted him. It came from a casket wedged among the rocks.

Atholle wrenched the casket from its resting-place and swam to the surface. The light shone upwards, beaming a path for him to follow until he came to the bright waters near the boat. As he burst through the surface, he closed the casket and handed it to Moorgate. He did not want to get back into the boat for he knew, that once he left the sea, he would become the same pathetic, ridiculous Atholle he had always been.

Moorgate hardly looked at the casket. He wanted to get Atholle back into the boat.

'No, I don't want to!'

'But everything you own is in here, your food, your clothes.'

'Maybe, but not what I am. I am happier here, and much smarter.'

'You don't want to be left on your own, do you?'

'Not really.'

'Come back into the boat, then.'

'I don't want to feel ridiculous. If I get back into the boat I will be ridiculous again.'

'You can always go back into the sea, for an hour or two. But you can't live there. You will be left on your own. You don't want that, do you?'

'Not really. I never liked living on my own and I suppose I would not like it now. If I get into the boat, promise you will never leave me. Promise, and don't fib.'

'I promise.' Moorgate put his hand out and helped Atholle over the side. At first he felt groggy, and then he began to feel ridiculous again. He asked Moorgate for a towel to dry himself with and put his clothes back on in the same silly way he always wore them. Then he did something Moorgate had never seen him do. He turned the lining of his pocket inside out and cried into it. 'I am silly. I am as silly as I have ever been.'

Moorgate tried to cheer him. But all Atholle would say was: 'The world is sad. It will always be that way. Open the casket and maybe all the misery will go away.'

Moorgate opened the casket.

Instead of a beam of light, an enormous sheet of flame spurted from the casket and engulfed the boat. But although the flame seemed to be all-consuming it did not catch fire.

The flame fanned up into the sky, lifting the boat, and Moorgate and Atholle with it. They drifted like a huge red cloud in which the boat, the oars, the casket, the trunkful of tools, the food pouches and the bamboo blow-pipe which Moorgate had hollowed spun around continuously. Moorgate and Atholle looked confusedly through the red-flamed curtain that tinged the sea and the sky with the blood of its fire. Sometimes they were flat on their backs. Sometimes they would be on their sides, then they would be bent almost double. Atholle saw the magic food pouches dip past him. He reached out and caught two of them and clutched them to him for dear life. Moorgate was struck by an oar and knocked unconscious, but it was no more than a few minutes before he was awake and alert again. Eventually they got themselves back into the boat, with the oars, food pouches, Moorgate's blow-pipe and trunkful of tools. The only object left floating was the offensive casket Atholle had unwittingly taken from the depths of the Great Ocean.

It had been hot in the gigantic cloud of flame, and they had to keep quenching their thirst from the pouch which held the wine. They drifted across the sky for eight days and eight nights. On the ninth day they were put down in a valley near the sea. They climbed stiffly from the boat. They looked at the sky, but the inferno of flame had gone; there was not a shadow of smoke or fire in sight.

At the time they did not realize it but they had arrived in Cromsutti, the Kingdom of the North. They were in a valley surrounded by rocky mountain slopes and precipes. Silver ribbons of waterfalls cascaded down the mountain cliffs but they could not see a river or lake into which the waterfalls drained. This puzzled them greatly. Eventually, having decided

that they would never be able to climb out of the valley as
the slopes were too steep, they got back into the boat.

Suddenly the ground opened and the boat fell down into
an abyss. They fell for a long time but the boat did not topple
over. It landed bottom first. Water splashed all around them.
Then the boat settled and surged off down a dark underground
tunnel which was full of a river in flow. They could hear
something hiss in the distance. It grew louder and louder as
the flow of the river brought them closer. Eventually, a pair
of green eyes loomed out of the darkness and Moorgate knew
that the eyes and hissing belonged to a dragon.

Atholle's teeth began to chatter and his heart almost fretted
away as they came closer to the sinister green eyes. Moorgate
groped for the blow-pipe but could not find it; somehow it
must have fallen overboard. He moved to the back of the boat
and dipped an oar into the river, using it as a rudder. He
pulled to one side in the hope the boat would pass out of
the dragon's reach. They could now see the dragon's jaws and
the outline of its scaly neck. But luckily it was head-on and
not lying crossways, blocking the tunnel. Miraculously, they
shot past it. It turned its head and shot out a bolt of flame,
the heat of which seared the wetness from their clothes in
a cloud of steam. The rumble of its rage echoed off the tunnel
walls as they were carried headlong by the swollen river.

Though they did not meet another dragon, other monsters
whirled and spiralled out of the water, mocking and tormenting
them until they were almost demented. There was nothing
they could do. They had to persevere, despite the flaunting
of the orcs, or water goblins, or whatever they were. One sat
on the oar which Moorgate was using as a rudder, a silly grin
on its face. Moorgate shook the oar but the goblin held firm.
Then he had an idea. He threw one of the berries he had
picked from the enchanted tree at the goblin. The goblin
greedily caught the berry and swallowed it. He gave a hollow
laugh of satisfaction, but the tone quickly turned to a whine

as he disintegrated, both body and voice a traceless entity.

Ahead of them in the distance they could see light. Gradually it became brighter. They made their exit from the tunnel into a canyon, past which the cliffs gave way to flat land. Far away to the right there were mountains which belched lava, and the sky was flecked with clouds of ash. But that was miles away.

The river widened and the flow became less hectic. Moorgate lit his pipe, settled back, and had an enjoyable smoke. The river was indeed proving to be a great river. Great as it was, though, it had no bridges. A river without a bridge was like a king without a crown. Where there were bridges there had to be roads. And people. But here there were neither bridges, roads, nor people; not between the river and the copper-coloured rocks; not betwen the river and the red fists of the mountains. But Moorgate was not too worried; they were bound to pass beneath at least one bridge before they came to the sea.

But Moorgate and Atholle never came to the sea. Unbelievably, although the river-flow was with them, the river became shallow and dried up. Moorgate said nothing to Atholle but he knew there was something seriously amiss. Rivers in flow just did not dry up.

They hauled the boat and their belongings on to dry ground. Atholle began to complain but Moorgate was too busy passing a shrewd eye over the dry lava landscape to heed his complaints. There was a hillock nearby and gradually it changed colour until a steady red glow emitted from its dusty environs. A trail of small black shapes rose up from behind it, something like the wavering of a kite. They were indistinguishable from a distance, but as they came nearer it could be seen that they were ravens. There were eleven in all; five flanked on each side while one kept to the centre.

The ravens came slowly at first, but eventually they swooped and perched among the small rocks only yards away from

Moorgate and Atholle. One of them had a casket clutched in its talons, and as it landed the casket fell to the ground close to Moorgate. It was the same casket which Atholle had taken from the depths of the Great Ocean. The ravens landed with their backs towards Moorgate and Atholle but when they turned around their beaky faces and feathered bodies were transformed. Instead of ravens, there stood wizards. Atholle turned deathly pale with shock. Moorgate steeled his nerve. He had dealt with wizards before and he was not overawed. The only matter that worried him was, which of the wizards was Nadair.

The wizards scowled and quickly surrounded the two of them. Moorgate had the good sense not to say anything and Atholle kept silent through sheer fright. The wizards marched them over the rough ground to the red hillock. A boulder rolled back and an entrance was revealed. They entered and found themselves in a building that looked like a temple. There were three altars on which had been placed a gold dagger, a wand, and a cross made from scented roses. Two circles set in the marble floor were inscribed, in gold lettering, with magic symbols.

The temple's most prominent feature was an ebony decorated vault with five doors. One of the wizards opened a door; inside there was a wax effigy of Moorgate. Another door was opened and an effigy of Ezon was discovered.

'Would you like to see one of yourself?' a wizard asked Atholle before adding, 'As soon as you do something to harm us we will make one of you.'

They said no more to Atholle; their interest was entirely centred on Moorgate. They glared at him and their thin lips quivered with rage. They pointed accusingly at him, and he had to stand back in case their long fingernails would scratch his face.

'Three doors left,' leered the wizards. 'Choose the right one and you will escape. But of the other two, one leads to madness, the other to death!'

Moorgate turned to Atholle and said, 'You have done no harm. Which door would you choose?'

It was clear that the wizards were annoyed at this turn of events. Looking dangerously venomous, they drew closer.

'This one,' chose Atholle. He turned the knob and the door opened without any effort. Moorgate ran in quickly, shoving Atholle in front of him. He slammed the door shut, hoping the wizards would not follow. But four did! They cornered Moorgate and Atholle and, drawing silver-tipped wands from beneath their cloaks, pointed them at the two captives.

Sparks began to spit from the tips of the wands, and at any second Moorgate expected them to strengthen into powerful rays that would pierce through both of them and burn them to a cinder. He reacted quickly; he tripped Atholle and both of them fell to the ground. The rays shot out over them, criss-crossed, and struck the encircling wizards who were burned to ash. Moorgate and Atholle got to their feet. A few seconds previously there had been eleven wizards; now there were only seven.

Moorgate and Atholle calmed themselves and walked on; at least they had not picked the door of death! They came to another door and walked through it. Now they knew that they had escaped from the wizards. They found themselves on a rocky plateau, with the evil red hillock still glowing behind them. In the background, mountain peaks spat fire and overflowed with rivulets of molten lava. Occasionally hot ash was blown towards them and fell in showers that they had to dodge. A little way on, they came upon a circle of lava. A circle of lava — with a familiar figure in the centre.

'I don't believe it!' said Moorgate. 'It can't be!'

But it was. It was Ezon!

Ezon leaped to his feet when he saw Moorgate and Atholle. He had used Morthern's sword in an attempt to escape from

the circle of lava, but its magical power of absorbing flame
had failed to work. Now his feeling of utter dejection vanished.
Moorgate would find a way out!

It was Moorgate who suggested that perhaps the sword's
power would be restored from outside the circle. Ezon threw
the sword and Moorgate held it with both hands as close to
the lava as he could venture. His idea succeeded. The bubbling
lava was drawn into the blade and Ezon was freed.

Atholle wanted to go back into the red hillock and torch
the wizards with the hot lava. Ezon shook his head.

'The remaining wizards will have disappeared by now. They
will have assumed their raven shapes and flown away. We
will have to wait for vengeance till another day.'

They retraced their steps through the plateau of lava until
they came to the place where they had left the boat. Magically,
the river which had dried up and forced them to abandon
the boat, was in full flood again!

When Ezon had eaten ravenously from the food pouches,
they pushed the boat into the river, and Ezon let the lava
in the sword flow over the river bank, where it sloped away
from the river. The lava flowed in a hot stream. It was an
impressive sight! Ezon sheathed his sword, took two heavy
oars and rowed, while Moorgate steered the rudder. The current
against them was very strong, but gradually, much to their
amazement, it ebbed and changed, flowing in the opposite
direction.

The boat carried them far from the wizards, the repulsive
goblins and the rage of the dragon. It got dark; then it got
bright. Day darkened into night, night lightened into day. They
travelled for three days until, at last, they came to a town
which was only a mile from the sea. Moorgate felt nervous
because he knew the people of the town were human people,
and the sight of an elf would only mean ridicule, which would
be compounded by Atholle's dress and odd behaviour. They
rowed in quietly beside a deserted wharf, and both Moorgate

and Atholle cut sorry figures as they climbed from the boat and hid behind whatever cover they could find, until they came to a derelict house on the edge of a wild meadow. They climbed in through a gap in the door, went up a rickety stairs and found a hiding-place in the loft, where they tried to make themselves as comfortable as possible.

Moorgate and Atholle peered through a slit in the loft. They could see a thin strip of the river and meadow. After some consideration they thought it better to go to sleep, so that when they awoke they would be fresh, to face the dangers which were steadily mounting against them.

They whispered 'Goodnight' to each other and fell asleep.

Ezon did not go with them. He strolled down along a path and into the town to find lodgings.

8. The Man in the Grey Suit

For weeks Patti and Simon knew they were being followed. Even when they went to the quarry a man in a grey suit trailed them; if that was not obvious nothing was.

'He's either a newspaper man or a scientist,' said Simon.

'He's not a scientist, because scientists are too busy experimenting to have time to follow people.'

'He's either a newspaper man or a scientists' spy, then.'

Simon was partly right. The man *was* a scientists' spy.

Dresus's second-hand car business was booming. He had a mechanic who wasn't interested in anything except car engines. He was very good — or so Dresus believed. He put old parts in car engines and took out new parts. He interfered with mileage clocks, and temporarily concealed rust marks. He did countless dishonest things, and he delighted in doing so. But he knew there would be trouble from dissatisfied customers, so he did not plan to stay in the job very much longer.

One afternoon on his way to the bank Dresus passed Patti and Simon. He stopped dead in his tracks; they looked at him blankly and walked on. He watched them go into a shop and edged close to the window so as to get a better look. He was puzzled at their failure to recognize him; he had held them captive long enough when he had been sovereign in his own kingdom. But gradually it began to occur to him that the two children in the shop were not the royal children at all; they were the two mysterious children who had ridden with Ezon and helped the royal children to escape from the island cavern where he had his impregnable dungeon. No wonder they had not recognized him! They had never seen him before.

He turned away from the window. He had a leer on his face. He would encounter the children some other time. And maybe he would kidnap them or . . . worse.

Late one autumn evening all the house and street lights went out in Oakten. Car lights failed and car engines cut out. For an hour there was chaos. Motorists were especially bad-tempered. After an hour all the lights came back on, the car engines splurted to life and everything returned to normal again. Just one of these things, rationalized everyone.

There was one other unusual occurrence, but nobody knew about it until the next day, and nobody cared anyway, except Dresus, alias Mr. McCoy. Two deep gashes appeared in the concrete forecourt of the car-sales lot; one was the image of a crown, the other the outline of a sword. Dresus knew what the indentations signified. Patti and Simon would have known too, but they seldom passed that way; it did not lie on their route to school.

Dresus had the two gashes filled in and cemented over. He sat in his office all day, a worried man. Once he had had a crown and sword, but he had never found out what happened to them. He had a gut feeling somebody powerful was trying to do him harm — somebody he did not like, and whose name he found detestable: MORTHERN!

9. Sikron Makes a Deal

Moorgate heard voices downstairs in the kitchen. He leaned over and woke Atholle. Together they crept to the trapdoor of the loft, and listened. There were two voices. One belonged to Ezon and Moorgate quickly recognized the other; it was Captain Sikron's. There was no mistaking the distinctive word-imagery of the old sea-dog. Ezon must have come across him in one of the town's taverns where, as likely as not, the Captain had been up to his neck in some devious plot. Although Moorgate had met Captain Sikron before, Atholle only knew of him by reputation; he had not particularly liked what he had heard.

Moorgate opened the loft trapdoor and quietly tip-toed down the steps. Ezon and Captain Sikron sat at a table in the centre of the room. There was a lighted candle on the table, and the yellow flame made the room dance with shadows. Moorgate, invisible in the darkness, listened as the voices drifted up towards him.

'It'd be cuttin' the tide from me stern,' came Captain Sikron's voice, his captain's hat held pincer-like in his calloused hands.

'There's no need for mistrust, Captain,' answered Ezon back.

'Aye, no need! No need to humble me more's likely. There's a black mark of vengeance in me heart. Aye, I can't forgive.' Captain Sikron spat out the words with venom. Once in the past Ezon had bested him and he still bore a grudge.

'That was your own doing, Captain.'

'Naw, 'twas yours. What I don't forget I don't forgive!'

'You were well rewarded for your humiliation.'

And in truth Captain Sikron had been well rewarded for the loss of face he had suffered at the hands of Ezon during the rescue of the royal children from Dresus's island dungeon. But the reward was gone now, squandered in the taverns of Cromsutti and elsewhere.

'You can trust me, Captain Sikron.'

'Split the jib-boom! The day I trust you'll be the day I rest me head top o' the main-sail. Naw, I'm not goin' to put me ship in danger. An' no one's goin' to tell Captain Sikron what te do, no one!'

'There is no danger. All you have to do is to arrange to take the children back to the East.'

'That's if ye find'm. I'd want a mineful a' treasure ... Maybe I'll do it if things work out well for ye. I'll have the *Atcheze* an' a few other ships ready to take the blighted unfortunates East. Aye, I'll do a bit, but only what's safe to do. This land's half a what's not human ...'

Suddenly Captain Sikron lunged into the darkness on the stairs, and, after a scuffle he dragged Moorgate into the candlelight. '... Haagh, a hairy hob-knob! Shiver me poop, it's the thorny runt of a elf, Moorgate! Sure's all elves look alike. Ye're Moorgate, are ye?'

Moorgate felt humbled. He nodded his head in affirmation, annoyed that Ezon was not in the least sympathetic to his plight. All he did was laugh. But Atholle was not long in coming to the rescue. He rushed down the stairs and kicked Captain Sikron in the shins. The Captain roared in pain and let Moorgate go.

'The kick o' a mule,' he fumed. 'If 'twas different times I'd splice yer liver. But yer among friends now. 'Tis easy the wind changes. D'ye know who I am? The elf knows. But d' you?'

Atholle hesitated before answering. 'Yes, I know who you are. You are a man who drinks too much. And there is as much wind in your stomach as there is in the sail of your ship during a storm.'

'Wha' ye say? Did me ears hear, or are me bells goin' barmy?

I bow afore nothin', not even the ragin' briny what's the biggest test o' a man's courage, ye snivellin' scarecrow!'

'I don't snivel. And I am not a scarecrow. I am of superior quality.'

Sikron roared again. He felt he was arguing with a fool. The insults got worse, and so did the tempers. Ezon had to step in between them to cool matters down.

'Atholle, fetch the wine pouch for the Captain.'

At first Atholle would not do as Ezon asked. His pride was hurt and he was not going to lose face. But at the mention of wine Captain Sikron's rage subsided somewhat and the situation became defused. Atholle sensed this and he grudgingly went to the loft and fetched the wine pouch. Luckily the Captain did not drink a lot from it, as he had none of his henchmen with him to carry him back to the *Atcheze* if he got too drunk. But he drank enough to hiccup and stutter, and rhyme a few uneven sea-shanties. He even picked Moorgate up and left him sitting on the edge of the table, saying, 'We'll let our little elf friend here dangle a jiffy while you and I discuss business.'

'Captain, can we rely on you to take the children back to the East?'

'That ye can, if ye find'm. If them wizards ever put an eye on me — me what's on'y a sea-captain — I think I'd be haulin' anchor an' settin' sail without ye. But if I'd stay in port while ye do the searchin' I'd not mind takin' the children.'

'Also, I want you to take us to the Ancients.'

Captain Sikron was taken aback. He did not really want to sail anywhere near the airless environment of the strange island where the Ancients dwelled. And if he did, he only had one hope; that the ship's anchor would hold firm, and that the *Atcheze* would not drift too close to shore and be caught in the suffocating airless vacuum of the island.

Just then a cock crowed and Moorgate gave a glance towards

the window. He wondered whether it was really a cock or
one of the wizards.

Shortly before dawn Captain Sikron agreed to set sail for the
Ancients. But first, the wizards would have to be pursued and
destroyed. And in reality there was only one person who could
do this — Moorgate.

10. A Message from Nadair

The loudspeaker in Mr. McCoy's used-car lot blared pop-
music. At intervals the music was interrupted by the
announcement of 'bargain cars at bargain prices'. There were
two loudspeakers on long poles at opposite sides of the forecourt.
Small triangular bunting, strung on yellow cord, circled the
forecourt.

Dresus had been out on the forecourt talking to a prospective
customer. The customer had lost interest and Dresus had gone
back to the office where he sat twiddling his thumbs. He was
still brooding about the appearance of the indentations of the
crown and the sword.

What did it mean? Trouble?

And trouble did come. First, the forecourt began to scar
with cracks. Then, the announcements about bargain cars
became garbled static. The static became so loud that it was
heard over most of Oakten. The police went in search of the
noise. Ordinary citizens also went in search. They all traced
it to McCoy's used-car lot.

When the static first started Dresus believed he could deal
with it. All he had to do was to turn a dial off. But the dial
got stuck. He roared to his secretary to help, but she could
not hear him. All she could hear was noise. All she could
see was Dresus's mouth pouting like a goldfish. Dresus put
his hands over his ears. He stamped his feet on the ground.

He roared. But nothing could be heard except the deafening screech of static from the loudspeakers.

Dresus ran outside. There was a crowd on the forecourt, but he ignored them. He wanted his mechanic urgently, to get him to switch off the noise. He threw open the door of the repair shed — and the whole world seemed to crash down about his ears. He fell flat on his back, knocked to the ground by pieces of a cooling system, piston-rods, a carburettor, springs of every kind, and an engine gasket — all the bits and pieces that were the stock in trade of the used-car trade. Some spanners and two hub-caps were blown across the forecourt and over the road, where they ended up festooning the traffic-lights. Naturally, the mechanic was not to be found. Luckily nobody, except Dresus, had been hit by the assortment of mechanical shrapnel; he was sore and blue and puffy all over. The fire brigade arrived, avoiding the cracked sections of the forecourt. A ladder was hoisted and a fireman climbed up and cut the wire leading to the loudspeakers. The static stopped immediately and a hush fell over the crowd. The fire-chief got up on the back of the fire-engine and shouted out something about magnetic fields.

One thing was certain; from that day on everyone who lived in Oakten became interested in Dresus and his used-car lot.

A week later Dresus's mechanic gave up his job. So too did his pretty secretary. Dresus was really down on his luck. Shortly afterwards the bottom really began to fall out of the business. The forecourt cracked open and there were holes everywhere. They did not all appear at once; sometimes a complete day passed without the ground opening and a car sliding, with a sharp metal clang, into the abyss. It was very hard to get the cars out and they were always badly damaged, with shattered windscreens, bent fenders, squashed wings and roofs, and mangled doors. And as car after car became a write-off Dresus became more and more distraught. In fact, he became quite deranged. In the end the forecourt became one

gigantic crater with a massive bellyful of cars that were only
fit for the junk-yard.

Dresus had not lost all his cars though. He had managed
to drive a favourite yellow car off the forecourt. He had only
learned to drive, and like all new drivers he wasn't very good
at it. But luckily he did not have to drive very far; only to
a plot of waste ground around the corner.

Dresus was not just having trouble with his cratered
forecourt. As the holes multiplied, so too did the number of
dissatisfied customers. Every customer to whom he had sold
a car came back to complain — came *walking* back! The cars
they had bought had all broken down and were complete
mechanical failures. Some of the customers were accompanied
by their solicitors. Others brought mechanics to verify the faults.
But most just brought their bare fists and threatened Dresus
that if they did not get their money back they would leave
him black and blue all over.

Dresus managed to ward off the disgruntled customers for
a few days, but before long his nerve broke and he knew he
just had to get out of Oakten. That was when he went to
the waste ground and drove off in his yellow car. But that
was not to happen until the following Thursday. In the
meantime he became almost crazy with worry. He consulted
a doctor who advised a visit to a psychiatrist. Secretly he
wondered if there was a wizard anywhere in the world who
would help him. But he dared not ask, afraid he would be
laughed at.

In the depths of his despair, he went to the roadworks where
he had emerged from the withered tree. Amid the rubble and
the dry cement scattered everywhere, he stood looking at the
spot where the tree had been, as if for inspiration or comfort
— or both. Nothing happened. After a while he looked
elsewhere, and under his gaze letters formed in the cement.
He watched them take shape. The letters extended into words!
It was a message! It said:

Kidnap the children, Patti and Simon.
Keep them hidden so as they can't be
brought here.

NADAIR

Patti and Simon? And then he remembered. They were the
children who looked identical to the Prince and Princess, Toria
and Panri — the two children he had recently seen going into
a shop. And they *did* look identical to the royal children. He
surely would recognize them again. And then, of course, he
most certainly would kidnap them.

A message from Nadair! He found the fact consoling. Perhaps
there would be more messages some other time. His spirit
lifted. At last he had made contact with the world from which
he had been exiled.

He got into his car and drove back to Oakten.

11. The Temple of the Wizards

The boat bobbed in the black cascade of the river, as it floated
strongly below the mountains of red and fiery orange. The
boat was not the elf-boat Moorgate and Atholle had journeyed
in before, but one of the long-shore boats from Captain Sikron's
ship, the *Atcheze*. Ezon and Atholle helped to steady the boat
with the oars while Moorgate held on to the rudder. Captain
Sikron was not with them; he had stayed down-river on board
the *Atcheze*, not far from the derelict house where Moorgate
and Atholle had spent the previous night. Now they were on
their way to confront the wizards.

When they reached the cleft where the river went
underground, Atholle warned of the goblins and the dragon.
But Ezon retorted grimly, 'I've dealt with dragons before. Lead
on!'

The boat lurched and shot forward into the black hole of

the cleft. All Atholle could remember was Ezon drawing his
sword and the boat settling back into the water, as the rapid
flow of the river sped towards where the dragon was waiting.
But the dragon and goblins were not there, and they passed
through the underground flow without incident.

When they came to the place where the river had dried
up before, they pulled the boat from the pebbled river-bed.
The hillock was still there but no longer glowed red. Moorgate
led the way to where he thought the entrance was. At first
nothing happened, but after a while a boulder rolled away,
just as before, and the entrance was revealed. As they walked
in, a yellow light swirled about them, and they could hear
a faint wheezy laugh. Moorgate pulled his elf's cap down over
his ears so as to blot out the laugh, but it got louder and
louder.

They walked through the door into the temple of the wizards,
and as they did, it slammed behind them and the wheezy laugh
stopped. The yellow light had gone too. Four enormous lighted
candles were positioned about the shrine so that it was in half-
shadow, half-candlelight. Smaller candles were placed in
clusters of four on separate tables. The ebony vault was still
there, all its doors closed.

Ezon knew a lot about wizards. He knew there should be
a silver bell somewhere. He looked more intently and there
it was! A small silver decorated bell.

'Which door did you escape through?' asked Ezon.

Moorgate pointed out the door and Ezon turned the handle,
but it seemed to be locked.

Just then a tinkling sound was heard. It was the silver bell.
It was floating in mid-air. Ezon clasped a hand to the hilt
of his sword. A wind began to blow through the shrine.
Moorgate's clothes billowed, and he felt the cold hands of
the wind pass across his face. For a few fleeting seconds he
saw and heard the elves of his native forest home dancing
and playing music in a wooded clearing. They were his brothers,

sisters and cousins. Just as quickly the apparition was gone. He knew it was a trick of the wizards, but there was nothing he could do about it. He felt a heavy sadness and a sudden longing to be in his forest home. He knew that the rage which was capable of building up inside him, and which could hurl out of him in a red spurt of fury would not do so if the wizards were to confront him now. His resistance was at its lowest ebb; his miserable state of mind had enfeebled his body.

Before Moorgate had time to dwell on the cunning of the wizards, three of the doors of the vault burst open, to reveal the effigies of Ezon, Moorgate and Atholle (who cowered back in terror). A weird multicoloured light shrouded the remaining two doorways and swirled just inside the thresholds. The bell rang and hovered beside each doorway, before floating back and settling again on one of the candlelit tables.

Then the wizards entered, dressed in white robes, flat white caps on their heads. Some of them laughed. Others spat and hissed. But they all chanted obscenities.

Ezon looked at Moorgate to see if the mysterious rage that had vanquished the wizards of the West was building up around him. But only sadness could be seen in his face. He looked forlorn and broken, and Ezon knew the wizards were working some kind of magic against him. Ezon steeled himself with a calm dignity. He drew his sword and told Atholle to keep out of the way.

'I have had enough of wizards' riddles,' he shouted. 'It is time you met what you cannot harm!' He lunged at the wizards with Morthern's sword. But although he struck with all his might the blows had no effect. The wizards turned into hoof-footed demons with bulging green eyes and scaly arms. Some even turned into freakish goblins and long-armed spiders that meshed a gigantic web and tried to entangle Moorgate in it. Three had turned into hopping lizards and were chasing Atholle, trying to snipe at his odd, loose clothes as he ran for his life.

Suddenly the whole shrine was struck by a tremendous bolt of lightning. The wizards stopped being demons and goblins, spiders and lizards. They became themselves again — seven dastardly wizards. But now they stood motionless, transfixed in the silver glow of the lightning. Then Morthern's voice boomed out: 'Evil has no right to prevail!' The wizards hissed and their faces bulged with rage. Ezon struck one of the wizards with Morthern's sword and he fell down, dead. He struck another and he, too, fell dead. A loud vibrating sound could be heard. The shrine began to quake and the three altars burst asunder. Ezon attempted to slay a third wizard but Morthern's sword was torn from his hand and floated upwards out of his reach. Then Morthern's voice boomed again: 'It is not for you, nor I, to slay wizards. Leave that task to whom it is decreed.' And with that, two sharp flashes of lightning criss-crossed and a blue afterglow enveloped Moorgate; the sadness drained from his body until a rage surged inside him.

The wizards knew exactly what was happening to Moorgate. They could see the red haze, the power bestowed upon him by the Ancients, build up around him, and they began to panic. The haze hung about Moorgate and then surged outwards. One of the wizards ran from the shrine and escaped from the red hillock. It was Nadair!

Just as he escaped through the boulder-blocked entrance a roaring wind blasted through the shrine. The doors of the vault slammed shut and opened again. They closed and opened and kept on doing so. Morthern's sword fell to the floor and Ezon snatched it to safety. A silver fireball shot through the shield of red rage which surrounded Moorgate. It burst asunder and darts of white lightning struck each of the wizards and the effigies in the doors of the vault. Morthern's voice boomed out: 'Put them through the door of the vault. Through the white door!'

Moorgate concentrated. He stood solidly as the wind howled, while the wizards and effigies were lifted off the ground and

mixed together, a solid mass of arms and legs and heads, as
they shot through the door of death. And the door was carried
with them, leaving behind a solid wall. It was as if the exit
had never existed in the first place.

Atholle was astounded, and perhaps a little vexed, Moorgate
should have told him in advance of the extraordinary powers
he possessed. Still he went over to him and hugged him as
tightly as he could. After all, Moorgate had saved his life and
Atholle, to be fair, was only showing his gratitude.

Morthern's voice boomed out once more, 'Nadair will not
forget you, nor will I forsake you, Ezon. You are to bring
Dresus's crown and sword and the two children who have
them, to the Four Kingdoms. The Ancients have decreed so.
The children will be needed to break the curse of the wizards
and to witness Nadair's downfall. Dresus will also succumb
in Nadair's fall from grace. The crown and sword are needed
to conclude the task. Moorgate will be the perpetrator, and
Nadair and Dresus will be forever incarcerated and bound
as one. The royal children, Toria and Panri, must also witness
the final downfall of Nadair and Dresus. So too Fraiter in
his capacity as the royal children's guardian. Everyone has
a part to play, Atholle included, if only as bait to ensnare
Nadair and end his lust for revenge.'

With that, the candlelight which had glowed throughout
the whole episode faded, and an image of the stone in his
father's shrine showed in one of the doorways. Ezon knew
exactly what the stone signified. He moved towards the door,
the stone receding before him. As soon as he went through
the door there was a blinding flash — and both Ezon and
the stone vanished. Above and below there remained only a
mist.

Moorgate and Atholle, who had been following Ezon,
suddenly found themselves walking on air. They wandered
on and on until, eventually, they could feel solid ground beneath
their feet and the glint of stars in the sky. As they stumbled

along in the darkness they could see the lights of houses straddling a small valley. They knocked on doors and asked for directions, but the unfriendly inhabitants only turned their backs on them.

They walked on into the night. Late the following day they came to the river and followed it to the sea, where the *Atcheze* was anchored just out from the wide wash of the estuary.

And all the time they wondered what had happened to Ezon and where he was now.

12. Kidnap!

Ezon, following the white and green speckled light which radiated from the stone, felt an unreal sensation, as if he were walking in a twilight world. Gradually the feeling of unreality ceased and the light from the stone dissolved until it was gone. So was the stone. And Ezon found himself in a green forest on the slopes of a dark mountain. He walked through the forest until he came to the slippery screed of the mountain-top. It began to rain, and then to thunder. Soon a storm battered over the mountain. A double flash of lightning criss-crossed and plummeted in a jagged arc over the mountain. Ezon lifted his hands above his head and the ring, once given to him in the shrine of the Ancients, shone with a red glow which lit up his whole hand and finally his body until, at last, a flash of lightning burst from the sky and struck him.

Everything was plunged into darkness. Ezon had disappeared. He had gone to do as Morthern had commanded — gone to bring Patti and Simon to the Four Kingdoms to take part in the struggle to free the children of the East from the evil clutches of Nadair.

The power of the ring had teleported Ezon to his father's shrine. He stood on the steps beside the marble column where the stone rested. He thought of going to Meridia, to tell her what was happening, but decided not to. She was totally unaware that he was there.

Ezon removed the stone from the column and placed it in a marble basin-like fixture full of water. When he placed his hands on the submerged stone the water bubbled and a milky light shone from the stone. It quickly cleared, leaving the surface of the water mirror-like. Living pictures began to form upon it — it was almost as if he were watching through a window.

First, Ezon could see Dresus emerging from the withered tree. Then there was the glare of car lights moving at speed in the darkness, and Dresus walking along the side of the road. The scene changed; now Dresus was stealing clothes from a clothes-line, putting them on and discarding his own. It moved on again, to a hoarding which read 'Oakten Welcomes Careful Drivers'. It was day-time, in a town, with cars, shops, and people walking about. Then it was Dresus again — Dresus, smartly dressed, standing on a forecourt surrounded by cars, with an enormously gaudy sign straddling the frontage: McCOY'S USED-CAR SALES.

Ezon was getting impatient. He wanted to see Patti and Simon. He wanted to speak to them.

Just then, the surface of the water clouded over, but in a few seconds it became clear again. Now he could see Patti and Simon. They were sitting in Patti's house watching television.

'Typical,' groaned Patti.

'Now, we'll miss the whole point of the story,' grumbled Simon.

The screen that the children were watching had suddenly become blank. A silver-like glow appeared, and a voice began to speak. It was a whole minute before they realized that it was Ezon who was speaking. It was uncanny!

Ezon cut through their cries of recognition and delight. His mission was urgent.

'You have Dresus's crown and sword, haven't you?'

'Yes, but we didn't realize they belonged to him. We found them beside a withered tree.'

'That withered tree held Dresus inside it.'

'You're joking!'

'No. You know what Moorgate did to Dresus, don't you?'

'Yes, turned him into a tree.'

'Well, there you are.'

'But that wasn't here. That was back with you.'

'Yes, but you found a crown and sword at the tree, didn't you?'

'Yes, we did.'

'That's proof enough. The crown and sword belong to Dresus and have to be brought back to the Four Kingdoms.'

'If Dresus was the tree,' said Patti, 'there's one very serious problem.'

'What's that?'

'The tree is no longer there; it is gone.'

'Yes, I know. He walked out of it and is living in your town.'

'Oh no!'

'If it is any help 'McCOY'S USED-CAR SALES' is written over the place where he works.'

'McCoy is Dresus! He is, isn't he, Ezon? There are all kinds of weird things going on at that car lot. If he recognized us we'd be in trouble. Ezon, you will have to help us.'

'You won't need my help — the Ancients will protect you.'

'But the Ancients are not here. How can they help us when they are not here?'

'They may not be there but their power exists.'

'What do you mean by that?'

'Exactly as I have said.'

'We don't even know what Dresus looks like. When we were with you we never met him.'

'Go to McCOY'S USED-CAR SALES and you will see what he looks like.'

'But, Ezon,' Patti's voice was anxious. 'Do we have to get mixed up in all this? It's all past and forgotten.'

Ezon paused for a second. Then he told them of the children who had been stolen from the East, and that it was part of the revenge that Nadair was wreaking because of the defeat that Moorgate had inflicted on the wizards of the West; the crown and sword were needed to seal Nadair and Dresus's fate forever. He also told them about Moorgate and Atholle and what had happened in the red hillock; how Morthern's voice had boomed out, and how he had followed the stone through the door of the vault. But when he mentioned that Morthern had commanded that Patti and Simon were to be brought to the Four Kingdoms, the children sat up in alarm.

'We won't go,' said Patti.

'In conscience you have to go. The missing children of the East are the same age as yourselves, and that is not just a coincidence. You were both involved in the events which led to the destruction of Dresus's army. You are part of the reason why Nadair is seeking revenge, and as such you have to come to the Four Kingdoms, if only to witness the moment the crown and sword are used to end Nadair's curse and destroy both him and Dresus. Anyway the Ancients have decreed it. You have no choice but to go.'

'They can't make us go!' But in her heart Patti knew they could make her go. And it was all because of the rings they wore — the rings which had the power to whisk them to the Four Kingdoms — just as Ezon's ring had the power to transport him instantly over great distances. They had often thought of throwing the rings away. But, once they had been placed on their fingers, they had never been able to remove them.

'It's not fair. It's a trap. We always thought the Ancients were good and would never do a bad thing.'

'Believe me, they are good, only sometimes their ways are strange. But good will come of it.'

'Not if we're gone for another fifteen years. Not if our parents are going to worry. We've suffered enough already. We can't go anywhere without being followed.'

'Followed?'

'Yes, we're always being followed, especially by a man in a grey suit. He's probably outside watching us now.'

'Why should anyone follow you?'

'Because they're suspicious, that's why.'

'Don't worry, they cannot harm you.'

'Maybe not, but it's very annoying . . . Ezon, when are we to go to the Four Kingdoms?'

'As soon as you fetch the crown and sword.'

'Well, that will have to wait until tomorrow. But let us ask you one thing . . . why can't the Ancients do something about all the years it will probably take? If they are so powerful why can't they make it look as if we were hardly gone at all?'

'I don't know. We could ask.'

'Who do we ask? Morthern? The Man in the Moon?'

'Atholle could ask.'

'Not Atholle! He's a joke!'

'Some jokes have a sting in the tail. You shouldn't treat him so lightly. Tomorrow, then. Bring the crown and sword and go to where the withered tree was. You can come to me from there.'

With that the dialogue broke off. Immediately the programme Patti and Simon had been watching flickered back on the screen but neither of them was interested. They switched it off.

As the children talked together, the full impact of what Ezon had told them finally began to sink in. They would have to go to the Four Kingdoms. They had no choice — the Ancients would force them if they refused. But they were worried about their parents. What could they tell them? How could they explain another absence? Their only hope was that the Ancients would do something to cancel the time difference. Why could Ezon not just have forgotten about them and left them alone?

That night neither Patti nor Simon slept; they could only think of what tomorrow might bring.

As for Ezon, the red glow seeped from the ring and he was gone from the shrine — gone to where the *Atcheze* was anchored, just out from the wide wash of a sheltered estuary.

The next afternoon, after school, Patti and Simon left home. They had the crown and sword wrapped separately in cardboard and heavy brown wrapping paper. They had said absolutely nothing to their parents about leaving, which made them both feel guilty.

What the children suspected about being followed was true. As they walked into town to get the bus to the quarry, a man dressed in a grey suit tailed them, and when they turned down a deserted side street, so did he.

Suddenly, a yellow car turned into the street and screeched to a halt beside Patti and Simon. The car door opened and out jumped Dresus. Before the children had time to react, he grabbed them and threw them into the back of the car, together with the crown and the sword. Hurriedly he jumped back into the driver's seat.

Simon opened the car door, shouting for help, but before he had time to jump out Dresus leaned over and pulled him back in. The man in grey seemed rooted to the spot — until he had to jump out of the way as the car veered across the street into a pole. The pole wobbled and a row of wires fell down on to the roof of the car. There was a blue flash and sparks shot up and bounced off the car roof. Then there was a flash from inside the car.

The man in grey could hardly believe his eyes. There were no longer three people in the car; there was only one — the driver! He lay unconscious, slumped over on the passenger seat. The children and the two large packages they had been carrying were gone.

A crowd began to gather. Someone rang for an ambulance, and a linesman to deal with the fallen wires which were still sizzling. A policeman arrived and enquired if anyone had seen the accident. The man in the grey suit said nothing.

When the live wires were dealt with and an unconscious Dresus taken away in an ambulance, the man in the grey suit went to the nearest public phone and rang his superiors. He told them the name of the hospital the crash victim had been taken to.

Dresus was not too badly hurt. He regained consciousness a few hours later; he was black and blue all over, and totally dejected. Three strange men came to visit him. They were scientists. They had a cassette recorder with them, and asked Dresus to speak into it. There was a doctor present as well. And none of them, neither the three men nor the doctor, was over impressed by the way in which Dresus raved.

'I am Dresus, King of the West,' he kept mumbling.

'Who?' asked one of the scientists.

'Dresus, King of the West. I lost my kingdom. Then my crown and sword ... the two children ... I lost everything ... And I have failed Nadair.'

'The man is raving,' whispered the doctor.

Then the three scientists consulted among themselves. One said, 'Don't forget there were three people in the car. Two vanished into thin air.'

'Yes, the two children we had under observation.'

'We might as well go to their homes and check them out. If they're not there and have gone missing again ... well ... we'll just have to wait and see, won't we?'

The three scientists left to go to Patti and Simon's homes with a view to checking them out. But lots of things were to happen. And, thankfully, they never got there.

As for Dresus, he raved on and on about being a king, and

knowing a wizard named Nadair. But of course there was
nobody by the name of Nadair in the telephone directory,
so the doctors had him certified and sent to a lunatic asylum.
There he raved about how all the cars in the world had broken
down and that he had been blamed for every last mechanical
failure because he had sold every car in the world.

To help him calm his nerves Dresus was given a job as
a gardener in the grounds of the establishment. And all this
seemed to happen on the same day. The day the car crashed;
the day he had woken up in hospital; the day he had been
committed to the lunatic asylum; the day he had been given
the job as gardener.

And then, also on the same day, Dresus vanished from the
lunatic asylum. Like Patti and Simon, he vanished into thin
air. And like the three men who left to go to the children's
homes and never arrived there, an awful lot was to happen
before Dresus would be heard of again. An awful, awful lot
— some of it wonderful, and some of it shocking.

PART TWO

13. The Island of the Ancients

The massive surface of the Great Ocean lay on all sides, from horizon to horizon. In the distance the skyline looked murky and grey. The *Atcheze* had been at sea for three weeks. She was becalmed and her sails hung limply, empty of wind.

The crew cursed their luck. They had worked hard at the menial tasks which Captain Sikron had set them. But the windless sails preyed upon their minds and the monotony of their daily routine gradually sapped their morale. Some of the men became lazy and neglected their duties. Some played cards, others lay day-dreaming in their hammocks, but perhaps the most remarkable indiscipline was the disrespect they showed Atholle. They goaded him when Moorgate was not about, and called him spiteful names.

What annoyed Atholle most was that the crew should have been in awe of him. They were on course for the Ancients, and Atholle was to set foot on the Ancients' airless island, a feat which had hardly ever been dared, and never before succeeded in by any living person. But instead of treating him with respect the crew ridiculed him, jeering the silly way in which he dressed and all the ridiculous things he said and did. They even stole his magic food pouches from him, and he would never have got them back only Moorgate went looking for them.

Eventually, Atholle could take no more. He complained to Moorgate, who was furious. The little elf told Atholle to hide his hurt, that there was a very simple solution. From that moment on Moorgate went everywhere on board ship with Atholle. The cut-throats and blackguards who comprised most of the crew found that the jibes had to stop. The simple fact was, they were afraid of Moorgate; they knew he was full of magical powers. Still, Atholle felt belittled. He sulked and

withdrew into himself, and Moorgate had to try very hard
to bring him to his senses.

Captain Sikron was just as bad as the rest, and if Atholle
had been on the ship on his own, the Captain would, more
than likely, have thrown him overboard and abandoned the
voyage to the Ancients.

Much as the crew feared Moorgate, they were absolutely
terrified of Ezon. But he had stayed below deck for most of
the voyage.

Eventually, the windless calm lifted from the sea, and the
deck-head lanterns swayed as the boom of canvas and the creak
of spars jostled in the following wind. After a few days they
came across jagged pillars of stone which protruded from the
sea-bed, and the ship had to manoeuvre carefully. An added
hazard in the form of fog now began to swirl and thicken
low over the sea. Very little could be seen from the deck.
A sailor had to climb the shrouds to the top-mast on to the
narrow bulge of the cross-tree, and shout down directions to
the ship's wheel on how to avoid the dangerous rocky
protuberances invisible from the deck. Hours were spent
piloting through the blanketing blindfold of fog. The crew
was certain the ship was going to founder, but, almost
miraculously, the fog lifted and they drifted away from the
danger, back to the passage of the open sea.

The pillars had been the cause of some concern to Captain
Sikron. He could find no mention of them on the ship's charts.
He had a dread of the supernatural and he was not sure which
frightened him more; the pillars, or the mysterious presence
which must have put them there — Nadair, of course!

Two days after passing the prongs of the pillars, a storm
arose.

'The sea an' the very winds o' the earth's upset,' muttered
Captain Sikron to himself. He stood alone on the quarter-
deck, the spray from the waves dripping from his face and
clothes. He often talked to himself, and did not find the habit

at all peculiar, for he liked his own company best. 'Aye, the sea an' the very winds a the earth's upset, not like the grim mask o' a man. No deceit . . . just bare ferocity!'

As the *Achteze* began to roll, the Captain shouted for the ship's wheel to be tied with heavy ropes and so prevent the steerage from spinning out of control. The sky had darkened and flashes of lightning burst directly over the ship. The masthead lit up and the wetness of the spars glistened for just as long as the lightning forked across the sky.

Captain Sikron cursed the storm and the violent sea. He roared like an enraged bull as he squinted through the tossing sea-spray in the narrow intervals between the bolts of lightning, glancing up quickly at the billowing sails, fearful, not for his own life or the lives of his crew, but for that of his ship. More lightning bolts pierced the sky and lit up the sea-sluiced deck, the great wash of broken waves battering off the bows and sending a showering of spray over the quarter-deck.

Just then, when the storm was at its height, Captain Sikron saw two swans fly into the lightning and tumble down on to the deck. He reached for his cutlass to run them through, fearing they were of evil omen and presaged disaster. But just as he reached the main deck Moorgate grabbed him by the arm and prevented him from killing them.

The swans lay on the deck, dazed from their fall. Gradually they stirred and changed form. The swans disappeared; instead Patti and Simon lay there, each clutching a package close to them. They stirred and opened their eyes, and as they stirred the storm ceased, the sky became bright, and the only glow came not from the lightning, but from the enchanted rings on their fingers which shimmered in a swirl of light that extended over their whole bodies. They were helped to their feet, the red glow evaporated and they were able to go below deck unattended.

Ezon got them bowls of hot, steaming soup, took their wet clothes and gave them towels to dry themselves with. Then they were given fresh clothes which were more suitable to the Four Kingdoms.

Captain Sikron was curious to know what the packages contained, and when he saw the crown and sword he recognized them as belonging to Dresus. He said nothing. He went away and got himself a jug of rum for company. He was worried. He had never seen swans fall from the sky before. Nor had he ever seen swans change into people before. The whole experience had been very disorientating.

It took another five days for the *Atcheze* to reach the island of the Ancients. As they approached the island cliffs, the ship's sails were furled and a dove was set loose from a cage. It flew uncertainly in a wide circle above the ship before making off for the island. All of a sudden it fell from the sky and crashed into the sea. Immediately Captain Sikron shouted for the ship's anchor to be dropped.

A hush fell over the crew as Atholle was brought out on deck, completely naked except for a strip of cloth around his loins. His skin was whiter than pale, and one of the crew shouted out, 'Give 'im 'is clothes back!' Atholle, flanked by Ezon and Moorgate, seemed uneasy and kept looking to Moorgate for reassurance. A long-shore boat was hoisted out over the side of the ship and lowered into the water. Two crew members clambered down a rope ladder and waited in the boat for Atholle to join them. While some of the crew watched the goings-on on deck, others kept a sharp eye on the anchor-chain and the distant landfall, to make sure they were not unknowingly drifting closer to the treacherous airlessness of the island's confines.

'What have I to tell the Ancients?' whispered Atholle to Ezon.

Ezon handed Atholle a scroll wrapped in a water-proof container. 'The message is in there,' he said.

'I do hope it's important, because if it is that means I am important too, and I will have to be treated with great respect.'

'You know it's important. Just don't lose it, or make any delay.'

'But I don't know what the message is.'

'You don't have to know.'

'I want to know. I have to know the message. I could open it up but I can't read. Maybe the Ancients will read it to me.'

'I have already told you what the message is.'

'Well, I have forgotten. I have a very bad memory. It's probably because I never went to school. Tell me again.'

So Ezon had to tell Atholle all over again.

It was a message in three parts. Ezon wanted to know where the missing children from the East could be found, and how the power of Nadair could be obliterated. The third part was due to Patti's insistence; she wanted the Ancients to use their power so that it would seem as if they had never been away from home.

'I am delighted you wrote it all down. Anyway, it's only polite to write. Who wants to be told when you can read it. It's so much more intelligent.'

The crew had by now become very hushed and quiet. There was no more jeering, no more smart remarks, as they eavesdropped on the short snatches of conversation between Ezon and Atholle. On the contrary, each and every member of the crew suddenly regarded Atholle in the highest esteem. He was going to swim to the island. He did not need air to breathe. Not one of the crew could swim, not even Captain Sikron. And if Atholle did not need air that meant he could swim underwater, even deep down among the murky depths where countless galleons had sunk.

Captain Sikron looked at him thoughtfully; he knew where several sunken treasures were located. As of now Atholle would always be welcome aboard the *Atcheze*, and no one would mock him. Captain Sikron would see to that!

With a last warning from Ezon that he was to swim directly

to the island and not explore the depths of the Great Ocean, Atholle climbed down the rope-ladder. He ignored the long-shore boat and plunged into the sea.

The crew tried to follow his progress, passing the Captain's spy-glass from one to the other, but it was hours later before they spotted him sitting on the copper-coloured shoreline — a shoreline on which no mortal had ever set foot before.

The island was not flat. Beyond the beach, which was scattered with loose coral grit and sea-shells, rose a cliff. Atholle walked to the base and found that the slope was gradual, but slippy. As he advanced the slope became steep but this caused him no problem as steps had been carved out of the rock. He walked up to the top and found himself looking across the high crown in the centre of the island. There was not a tree, nor a plant nor a blade of grass anywhere. The whole island was one barren mass, encircled by the breaking sea-surf on the speckled coral sands.

Atholle plodded on and shortly came across a grey metal disc-shaped monstrosity, partly welded to a flat base on the ground. He halted, undecided what to do. A pathway of metal steps led downwards. He went down the first few, and found himself underneath the body of the disc. Looking up, he saw a separate series of steps, leading up as far as the belly of the disc, but there was no doorway, hatchway or entrance of any sort. He continued to follow the downward steps, which led to a passageway in the ground. It twisted first one way, then another; a few more steps, then another bend. He could hear whirring sounds which gradually became louder, and light began to flood the passageway. A final turn and he was in a huge cavern which contained all kinds of stairways and gantries, machines, instruments and sophisticated furnishings and fittings. It was the size of a small village.

And there were people — at least a hundred of them — only they were not human. They were only half normal size and really did not have bodies; but they had plenty of arms

and legs — well, they only had two each but they were very, very long, much longer than their small bodies which were no bigger than footballs. Their heads and necks were very big, at least three times the size of Atholle's. Their ears were big as well. But they did not have any noses, and their mouths were small and round. When they saw Atholle coming, they stopped whatever they were doing, and almost all of them gathered around him. They spoke a strange gibberish. Some of them touched him. It was not like being touched by ordinary people. A tingle went through him. It went from his feet to his head, but it did not last long. It was like sparks sizzling and then fizzling out.

One of them spoke to him: 'Are you Atholle?'

'Yes . . .'

'There is no need to be afraid . . .'

'I am not afraid.'

'Atholle, there is no need to tell lies. You are among friends. We are the subordinates of the Ancients. We call ourselves the Subservients . . .'

'We are all your friends . . .'

'How is that? I've never met you before.'

'Once you did. When you were very small . . . Atholle, you are one of us.'

'How? How? I don't look like you. I don't have a big head or big ears.'

'In part, you are one of us. You would not be able to survive in this environment if some little part of you didn't belong to us.'

'Oh dear! You mean I've got something you have got?'

'Yes, the same breathing system.'

'That's not much.'

'Perhaps not, but it is unique to us.'

'You're not related to me, are you?'

'No.'

Looking at their heads and ears and mouths, Atholle was

about to say 'Thank God', but he decided it might offend them so he said nothing.

'You grandfather was one of us . . .'

Another of the Subservients spoke and what he said shook Atholle to the very heart: 'Your grandfather's ancestors brought us here many thousands of years ago. But shortly after you were born he died, and all belonging to him was destroyed, including your father and mother.'

Atholle was heartbroken. It was the cruelest thing he had ever heard in his life. A great flood of tears overwhelmed him and he lay down on the ground and wept.

'That,' continued the Subservient, 'was why you were brought to Morthern as a child . . .'

'Ah,' said Atholle angrily, jumping to his feet. '*That's* something I want to talk about. Morthern dumped me on an island, on my own, and told me to look after a silly old Dial.'

'The Dial is not silly, and Morthern is just. The Dial has to be kept by a custodian, and you are that custodian.'

The Subservient spoke so sharply that Atholle was crushed. He decided to change the subject.

'I almost forgot. I am on a mission. I have been sent to you.'

'Nobody is sent, except by the Ancients. Whatever your mission is, tell us, and we will pass it on to the Ancients.'

'I have a message. Here it is. It's a very long message.'

One of the Subservients opened the scroll, and the more senior gathered around and debated its contents.

'We know Ezon has brought two children from another world . . . the time lapse . . . they want the time lapse stalled . . . that can be done. . . . We know of the wizards and their lust for revenge; they are all dead — sorry! taken care of — all except Nadair . . . . And the missing children of the East. Yes, they can be found. We will give you a map showing where they are held captive. But you will have to go to an old man, the sailmaker Gadua, and collect a compass which has powers that, when allied to the map, Nadair cannot interfere with. Gadua lives in a sea-town called Malstorn.'

'I couldn't remember all that. Write it down for me like Ezon did.'

'Listen . . . then you might remember . . .'

'I couldn't possibly listen. Write it down.'

'Very well, but first: The sailmaker takes care of a child who has certain divine powers. The child's name is Charbonne. Bring him with you on your quest. He will be needed. The crown and sword which Ezon took back from this other world are to be left in the garden of the castle near where the missing children are held . . . the sailmaker will tell you where this is. Ezon, Moorgate, Charbonne, Patti, Simon, Fraiter, and the Royal Prince and Princess, are all to enter the garden which is part of Nadair's castle-stronghold. There the evil powers of Nadair will be laid to rest for all time.'

'Quick, write it down. I have forgotten half of it already.'

'You are very feeble-minded. Do try to concentrate.'

'Be patient,' said another voice.

'Patient? I have always been patient. But my patience wore out a year ago. Write the message down. It is too complicated, even for a person cleverer than I.'

'But first, you will come to another castle. Nadair will be there. Make sure Ezon has Morthern's sword with him. He will need it. Nadair will come raging forward in the form of a dragon.'

'Nadair will be a dragon?'

'Precisely. But only until Ezon slays it.'

'Oh dear! Then he will be something else?'

'Yes; it will be part of the progression. The next encounter in the castle garden will finally put an end to him.'

'Will I have to go into this wretched castle?'

'No.'

Atholle felt relieved.

'Also remember: Tell Ezon that the royal children will be in the valley near the first-mentioned castle.'

'Ezon never told me they were held captive.'

'They are not. But they will come from the East with Fraiter. They, Moorgate, Patti, Simon and the dragon Celfy, who lives in a cave in the valley, are all required to lay at rest the final curse of the wizards.'

'I'm getting muddled,' said Atholle irritably. 'Quick, write it all down; it might straighten itself out.'

'That is all being done,' said another of the Subservients. He pointed towards a machine which had printed words coming out of it on a thin strip of paper.

'Is it all on that?'

'Yes.'

Atholle felt great relief. There was far too much to remember. He felt that he could not possibly listen to any more. It was very convenient to have everything written down so neatly. All he would have to do was to hand the long too-complicated-to-remember message to Ezon.

'Can you scold Morthern for being so cruel to me?'

'He has not been cruel to you.'

'He brought me to that island and left me alone for years.'

'That island is your purpose in life.'

'Well, it's not a very nice purpose. I want a different one.'

'It's not for any mortal to pick and choose.'

'I thought you said I was one of you.'

'You are still only a mortal.'

'It's not fair. Just because I'm me, I am treated any old way.'

'You are not treated any old way.'

'Well I feel I am. From experience I am. And experience is what counts.'

'Be satisfied with your life. Even to be standing here is something that has been granted to no other mortal. In that sense you are above everybody, kings included.'

Atholle felt slightly mollified, though privately he did not think much of the honour. He did not really want to be standing there. He would have much preferred to be a king, but he did not tell the Subservients that. And then he remembered something he just had to ask, something of the utmost importance.

'I would like to meet the Ancients.'

There was a long pause. When the Subservient spoke again, his voice was hushed: 'No living person can look upon the Ancients, not even those of us who serve them. We liaise with them through robots and computers. They are mysterious and reclusive. To look at them would mean certain death.'

'You mean they would kill?'

'No, it is part of their body force. By looking at them you would die.'

'Well, in that case, I suppose I don't really want to meet them.'

Then the Subservients told Atholle things about themselves, half of which he did not understand. He scratched his head and wrung his hands together, clenching and unclenching them and muttered the same short few syllables over and over: 'Oh, dear . . . Oh, dear . . .'

These new revelations were even worse than the message to Ezon, all terribly complicated and messy with detail. He could remember hardly anything — and whatever he did remember was confused and muddled. It was not fair. The Subservients should have written it all down, and Ezon or Moorgate could have read it to him. It would have been like a history, a history that had so many pages that Ezon and Moorgate would have got tired of turning the pages over.

He must have stood there for nearly an hour listening to what the Subservients had to say. Not that all of them spoke, only a few did, and he was thankful for that, because they liked to talk a lot, and if all of them had got a word in he would have been there for ages listening and hardly

understanding a word. Not indeed, it must be confessed, that
he listened all the time. He began to worry about Nadair and
dragons and evil curses. Could Ezon and Moorgate really crush
the power of evil? Could anything go wrong? He shuddered
to even think about it. It was all too worrying ... and all
the time the machines whirred and coloured lights flashed on
and off.

Eventually, he got fed up and said it was time for him to
go. So the Subservients brought him from the grey monstrosity
and out on to the crown of the copper-coloured hill. They
led him down the slope, back on to the beach, making sure
he had the map and their message for Ezon with him. They
left him standing knee-deep in the Great Ocean. They said
nothing, not even good-bye, and returned up the slope of the
copper hill.

They left Atholle on his own to swim back to the *Atcheze*,
a poor confused wretch who had never known his mother or
father. He felt all alone in the world, and he cried his eyes
out. He was not himself for days. But much to his credit when
the crew asked him what the Subservients looked like, he would
not tell them. Not even Ezon nor Moorgate were told. The
Subservients had looked so terribly ridiculous, and he was not
going to have them ridiculed. He knew too much about jeers
and hurt to wish taunts to be hurled at anybody, much less
the Subservients.

Likewise, when Ezon read the message from the Ancients
he would not tell Captain Sikron what it contained. But he
showed Moorgate the map. It was outlined on a yellow
parchment with tiny thongs of leather decorating the edges.
The markings kept changing position, and whatever lettering
it bore kept leap-frogging backwards and forwards making it
impossible to decipher.

There was only one solution, and that was to go to Malstorn,
to the sailmaker Gadua, and ask for the compass so that the
map would settle and they would be able to read it. And there

was also the vital participation of the boy, Charbonne, without whom the quest could not be successfully concluded.

There was a lot to be done, and Ezon had the resolve to see that the prompting of the Ancients was carried out.

14. Charbonne

Malstorn was situated in a fiord twenty miles from the sea. Captain Sikron had often sailed there before, and he piloted the *Atcheze* with ease through the deep trough of fresh water which lapped the base of the narrow cliffs. The fiord had an echoing effect, and when an order was shouted the noise multiplied and rang off the green forest cliffs like peels from a bell. When they neared Malstorn the fiord widened and swept into an arc, forming a wide, sheltered bay.

It was a picturesque place, with red-roofed houses along the shore and small fishing boats in the harbour. Big ocean-going ships anchored outside the harbour. Behind the low-lying town mountain peaks towered. The mountains held gold and diamonds; danger and mystery, trolls and dragons that spat fire; greedy adventurers who would kill for a lode of gold. And the mountain-tops were not all snow covered; some smouldered with lava, a trickle of black smoke marking the sky over the bubbling crust.

When the *Atcheze* berthed, Ezon asked Captain Sikron to go into town with him and try to find Gadua, the sailmaker. But the Captain was hesitant because of all the people he had cheated there in past visits to Malstorn. He feared fools might no longer be fools; that drunks might now be sober; that adventurers might now have tired of excitement and become aware of reality. He was afraid he might be remembered in Malstorn and that his victims would want to settle old scores.

But he need not have worried; those who had suffered at his hands had either left the town or died in the mountains.

Ezon and the Captain enquired in the taverns about the whereabouts of the sailmaker, but no one would tell them. They got the same result when they mentioned Charbonne's name. They also asked on the streets, but there too, there was silence. It was obvious that the people of Malstorn feared the sailmaker and the child, Charbonne; Ezon and the Captain were only wasting their time enquiring.

At one stage in their travels, they noticed an old woman, bent and wizened, watching them from the shadows of an alleyway. They paid no heed to her and walked on. They were to come across the same old woman again, but not for days, and under very different circumstances.

A blond-haired boy began to follow them. They halted and asked him why.

'Because you are looking for me.'

'You must be Charbonne, then?'

The boy nodded. 'Come I will take you to Gadua.'

They followed him through a maze of laneways, down a sloping path towards a river. They could see the sailmaker's yard from the slope, and noted its easy access to the waterfront. The sailmaker was there, standing outside his cottage.

Ezon introduced himself and Sikron. 'We are here to ask you for a compass which is needed for us to read a very special map.'

'This map, it comes from the Ancients, doesn't it?'

Ezon, slightly taken aback, said nothing.

'I know it comes from the Ancients. Have you ever heard of the Corvey?'

'No, who are they?'

'They be demons!' quaked Captain Sikron.

'They are phantoms,' corrected Gadua, 'who exist in a dream-world which only children can enter, and all they possess is phantom in substance. At Nadair's request they stole the children you seek from the East and took them to a place I will show you on the map. Charbonne will enter their world

and ask them to help. The Corvey are very fond of Charbonne
and they will do as he asks.'

The old sailmaker paused. A feeling of unease came over
Captain Sikron. He cursed a silent oath and wished he had
never set foot in Cromsutti.

Gadua then told Charbonne to go into the house and fetch
the compass. Not only that, but he was to bring out a spear,
a bow and a quiverful of arrows, as Ezon had lost his at sea
and it was time he was fully armed again.

Ezon was perplexed. 'How do you know so much about
me?' he asked.

Gadua refused to give an explanation, except to say, 'Many
the heart is light when kept in ignorance. Keep it that way.'

Charbonne came back with the compass and the weapons.

'The map has to be read carefully,' explained Gadua, placing
the compass on the opened folds of the map. Immediately
the markings and lettering settled. He pointed out the details
of the route Ezon would have to take to the vast mountain
range, called the Flante, where the children were held and
subjected to the cruelty of Nadair. When he finished he folded
the map and handed it and the compass to Charbonne,
instructing him to give them to Ezon along with the bow and
spear.

'The compass is part of a powerful circle,' he explained.
'Don't allow your hand to complete it. When your quest is
nearing completion, give the compass to Charbonne; he will
complete the circle by bringing the compass back to me.' Gadua
then invited Ezon and the Captain into his house. He talked
away as they stepped between the loose sail canvasses and the
ribbed splices of wood which some day would be the sails
of ocean-going vessels and river-boats alike.

The house was full of manuscripts. The old sailmaker invited
them to sit down while he skimmed an eye over a ream of
parchments on an oak desk. He took a blank sheet and wrote
on it. The writing was in symbols and Gadua studied it for

a while before speaking:

'The children are near a castle in a valley below the peaks of the Flante. You will travel there with the crown and sword you have in your possession. You, Ezon, and whoever accompanies you will travel overland, using the map. Charbonne and the two children you have in your company on board the *Atcheze* will travel to the Flante through the dream-world of the Corvey. There will be many dangers, but not for Charbonne or the two children, as anyone who enters the dream-world cannot be harmed.

'What will happen in the valley below the Flante will become more apparent later, and because the Corvey are torn between good and evil they will, when asked by Charbonne, take the enslaved children back to the East through the dream-world. Morthern, too, will be striving to do all he can to help. Fraiter and the royal children will come from the East.'

Gadua slowly pushed the parchments to one side. 'I am tired,' he said. 'Take Charbonne with you. I have no further use for him; not until your quest is completed.'

Gadua led them outside and watched them go up the slope to the laneway. Then he turned and walked back to the house. He had seen Charbonne go off many times before, and the boy would tell him all about his latest adventure with the Corvey on his return. Perhaps he would write it all down and put it away among all the other events of history which he had been privileged to record over the years. Perhaps he would; but only if it proved worth doing.

The old woman who had watched them from the shadow of the alleyway was still there, watching. She looked pitiful and forlorn.

And in her own time she plodded after Ezon, Captain Sikron and Charbonne.

15. Through the Dream World

Patti and Simon walked with Charbonne through the torch-lit streets of Malstorn, the twilight closing into full darkness in a matter of minutes, until they came to the empty blackness of the countryside. Then Charbonne took them by the hand and indicated they were not to utter a word. All of a sudden daylight was all around them and they realized they had entered the dream-world.

Spiky balls of fluff blew along the hunched hedgerows of the narrow field they found themselves standing in. Very quickly both fluff and field were gone; a forest had sprung up out of nowhere, and they were right in the middle of it. They were both frightened by the suddenness of the change. They felt a tossing sensation in their stomachs, something like going over a hump on the road in a very fast car. A path stretched before them, and they followed it through the forest until they came to a clearing. They could hear voices and music; they crept closer, then they hid and watched. What they saw were nine elves, who were in mourning for a dear friend who had gone and left their forest home. Charbonne explained that the scene they were watching was thousands of miles away, and that the dream-world could see and go anywhere in the Four Kingdoms.

One elf said, 'Moorgate's gone forever.'

Another said, 'He's become famous and doesn't want us any more.'

A third said, 'We shouldn't have been so hard on him. He wouldn't have gone away in the first place if we hadn't told him to brush the forest clear of leaves.'

Simon realized that he had seen the elves before. They had been with Moorgate the first time Ezon and Simon had ever met him, and the elf had left the forest with them on their great adventure to rescue the royal children, Toria and Panri. He felt terrible. He wanted to rush out of the bushes and tell the elves the real reason Moorgate had never gone back to the forest. The meek, considerate elf had not wanted the tranquility of his elf-folk disturbed by his new-found fame. Too many curious strangers would have come to the forest to congratulate him. Instead he had gone to live in seclusion with Atholle on an island in the middle of nowhere. Simon so much wanted to tell the elves that Moorgate was safe, and that he often thought of them; that he bore no malice towards them; that he missed them very much, and that he loved them.

He walked into the clearing. The elves did not run. They were not afraid. They stood looking at him, almost as if nothing had happened. Charbonne and Patti followed Simon into the clearing, and Charbonne whispered to Simon, 'Although they see us, it is not real to them. It is like in a dream, Some will remember, others won't.'

Simon told the elves that Moorgate was safe and happy, and that, maybe, some day he would go back to his forest house for a visit. The news cheered the elves no end, and they began to ask questions.

'Where does he live?'

'On an island.'

'Oh, that's lovely! An island! How beautiful.'

'Does it have trees?'

The questions went on and on. And with each answer the elves became more delighted and responsive. They drew around in a circle and linked arms, keeping Charbonne, Patti and Simon to the centre, and they danced. A few of them took out tin whistles, while a few more had fiddles and bows. One or two spread polka-dot handkerchiefs on the ground and danced around them. They all laughed and sang. After a while they became quite breathless, especially the dancers, who danced so fast that the polish and buckles of their boots became a blur. Then they called a halt, and had a quick drink and a

sandwich from one of their number, whose sole purpose in
life seemed to be that of drinks and sandwich carrier.

The buffet over, they took up the dance again. Then Simon
danced on his own around the polka-dot handkerchiefs, while
they all stood around, either playing instruments or clapping
hands. Then they asked Simon to play the fiddle, and
afterwards, a tune on the tin whistle. Finally they took the
instruments from him and shook hands, before vanishing into
the forest to further their search for a home, because wood-
elves were what they were and were always in need of a home,
especially one made from a human person.

Charbonne, Patti and Simon stayed a while longer in the
clearing, but gradually it disappeared and they were left
standing outside a house surrounded by a high wall. The hall
door was open and they went in. Inside there was a room
with three mahogany chairs beside a table — and an enormous
mirror on one of the walls. But the mirror did not show their
reflections — not quite! Instead it showed the royal Prince
and Princess, Toria and Panri, walking through a palisade and
into a cobbled yard. Fraiter was in the yard holding the reins
of two horses, one black, the other white. Patti and Simon
recognized the horses instantly. They were the same two
enchanted horses on which they had flown through the sky
the time Toria and Panri were rescued from Dresus's island
prison.

They could hear Fraiter talking to the Prince and Princess
as clearly as if they were standing beside him. Seemingly
Morthern had been in contact with Fraiter and told him to
take the Prince and Princess, along with the enchanted horses,
to Cromsutti to help destroy Nadair's magic spells and free
the missing children from his custody.

Then Panri spoke: 'It will be good to meet Moorgate, Patti
and Simon again. They risked their lives for us. They are
very dear friends. And perhaps we will see our dragon, Celfy.'

Just then the mirror clouded and everything faded.

Charbonne went over to the table and sat on one of the chairs. As soon as he did so, they saw that two ghost-like figures were sitting on the other two chairs. They had not walked into the room, or across it — they had come out of nowhere! One second they were not there; the very next they were sitting at the table with Charbonne. Although they wore clothes they looked like skeletons, only they had green eyes and lips. All of a sudden they vanished, just as quickly as they had appeared. Charbonne stood up immediately. The table and chairs began to float in the air. Then the chairs rocked backwards and forwards.

'Let's get out of here,' shouted Patti.

'No, stay!' Charbonne was adamant. He was not acting like a boy now. He had spoken with the authority of a man.

'I want to get out of here, it's terrible!'

'Stay where you are. We cannot be harmed!'

Green eyes looked out from an open door at the side of the room. The door closed. Then it opened. There were lips beneath the eyes. The door closed, and stayed closed.

The back door opened, and fresh sunlight spilled over the threshold. Patti and Simon ran for the door and Charbonne went after them. He did not want to leave them on their own.

Outside there were high walls everywhere, set out in the shape of a maze. Eventually, they came to a dead-end. Part of the wall burst open and a cascade of red cinders flowed out. There was a sword among the cinders and Charbonne kicked the cinders away from it and waited for it to cool.

Another section of the wall cracked open and the gap expanded until a door formed. Charbonne picked up the sword and brandished it. He opened the door and went through, followed by Patti and Simon. They were in what was left of the wizards' temple, the dull heavy shape of the vault before them. Charbonne struck the sword off the doors of the vault, and as he struck they burst into flame; that is all except the last door. He did not strike it; not until they had opened it and walked through.

'That's what the sword was for,' said Charbonne, 'to torch the wizards' temple.' Behind them the temple was a burning inferno, and Patti and Simon knew the sword must have come from Morthern.

Charbonne led the way out, the sword held aloft in his hand. They had no idea where they were and they kept on walking until it got dark. They looked up into the sky, above where the moon shone, and they could see the tiny plumes of silver stars trailing the black void. They came to an outcrop of rocks piled on top of one another and they decided to shelter there. Some loose wood was lying scattered on the ground. They gathered it and lit a fire. Charbonne left the sword lying on the ground beside him. They sat and talked, and some time during the period of conversation the sword shot into the fire and disintegrated in the flames. They marvelled at the sight, and, as the last flames expired from the fire, they stretched out and fell asleep.

They slept well into the next morning, but when they woke up the place where they had laid down was gone! When they stood up there was nothing beneath them. They were high in the sky. Mountains, plains, valleys, and the slack ribbon mark of rivers passed below them. The toss of their hair ruffled in the strong air-flow. They shielded their eyes. They could see a small shape in the distance moving towards them. As they watched it grew larger and larger until, finally, it became two horses and their riders gliding through the sky. The riders were Toria, Panri and Fraiter, and they had the insignia of the East emblazoned on their tunics. They passed close by but did not seem to sense the presence of Charbonne, Patti or Simon.

Patti was distressed that the horses — their horses — had passed them by, but Charbonne explained, 'They're going to the place where the children of the East are prisoners.'

'Why can't they see us?'

'Because they're not in the dream-world.'

'How do they know where to find the children?'

'Because Fraiter has found out. Clues have been left for him. Probably by Morthern.'

Fraiter, the Prince and Princess soon disappeared in the distance. Charbonne, Patti and Simon were enveloped in a cloud and found themselves back on solid ground; back where the camp-fire had been. It was night-time again and four phantom shapes sat around the fire, the glow from the embers passing in flickers through their skeleton bodies. They looked exactly like the skeletons who had so mysteriously appeared in the house beside the maze. This time Charbonne explained who they were. They were the Corvey. They seemed friendly towards Charbonne, who sat at the fire with them. Patti and Simon did likewise, though the Corvey completely ignored them. The children were glad; they did not want to have to look at those horrible skeleton faces. One of the Corvey scooped his hands into the fire and took out a crown and sword, the same crown and sword Patti and Simon had kept at home and which they had brought back to the Four Kingdoms. They were splendidly perfect; neither was burned nor tarnished by the fire.

Then the Corvey spoke, one at a time. Their jaws and lips moved, and they waved their skeleton hands. This is what they said:

'This is an illusion. But you, Charbonne, live in reality. There is a crown and sword to be placed where a tree will sprout from seed we will give you. The seed is to be placed in the garden of a castle which you know little about.

'You will meet, along with Ezon, Moorgate and Atholle, a group of knights cursed with an affliction.

'The knights will bring you to the castle where the seed is to be thrown on to the soil of the garden.'

The Corvey said no more. They threw the illusion of the crown and sword back into the camp-fire. One of them then

took a locket from the fire.

'This locket is for you, Charbonne. It holds the seed the tree will sprout from. Let Moorgate sow the seed and place the crown and sword in the boughs of the tree which will sprout from the seed. Then tell Ezon to touch the tree with the red jewel ring he wears. The tree will vanish and Dresus will be standing in its place.'

'Dresus!'

'Not him!' whispered Simon, but no one seemed to have heard him.

'We will have horses saddled for you and for Ezon's friends, for the journey is long.'

Charbonne expected the Corvey to say more but they had finished speaking. They handed him the locket before walking into the dark shadows of the night. The fire lost its glow and then it too was gone. But Charbonne and the children did not notice; they had fallen asleep.

When they awoke they were gone from the dream-world. They were now in the valley below the mountains, where all the prophecies of the Corvey were to be enacted. But they were not alone. Six bridled horses grazed close by. They crept up to them and snatched at the reins. Then they rode off through the funnel of the valley, hoping to meet up with Ezon, Moorgate and Atholle, and then continue on to rescue the missing children.

Little did they know that Nadair was watching from afar.

16. Creatures of the Mountain

Ezon, Moorgate and Atholle had many adventures on the long trek to the Flante. Twice, through his own pompous stupidity, Atholle managed to get lost and he had to be rescued. His magical food pouches also proved to be a hindrance. They were too cumbersome to be carried a long distance, yet he refused to allow Ezon or Moorgate to share the load. He wanted to carry them by himself, and it exhausted him. Eventually he agreed to bury the pouches, all except one, and retrieve them on the return journey. After all, Moorgate had left his chest of carpentry tools on board the *Atcheze* and Atholle considered that a bigger risk than burying his precious pouches in the wilderness. He chose not to bury the wine pouch as he remembered Morthern once saying that water was more essential than food for survival. Well, wine was not water, but at least it could quench a thirst. Anyway, they did not really need the other pouches as there was plenty of wild game and Ezon was a very adept hunter.

Not only was there game; there were also wild horses, and Ezon managed to get close to one and leapt on to its back. The horse bucked, but Ezon held on by its mane until it became subdued. He then coaxed Moorgate and Atholle to mount behind him. It was great to have the horse, especially as Atholle was not used to walking long distances, and Moorgate, because of his small foot-stride, was really walking three times as far as the other two, and, although he did not complain, his legs ached. Yes, the horse certainly made a great difference. But after the fourth day it was gone. It bided its time and galloped off back along the long miles to the rest of the herd.

Only one adventure of consequence occurred which related to their quest. That was after they entered marshy bogland on the edge of a great plain at the far side of which they could see foothills, and beyond the hills the peaks of the Flante. The boglands were eerie, and the marks of some strange animal that Ezon could not identify led through the swampy ground. They could actually see the hoof-marks being made; they were imprinted before their eyes as they walked along, as if some invisible animal were plodding along in front of them. When they came to the firm ground at the edge of the plain, the marks stopped beside some coarse bushes and bracken. Ezon's senses told him that danger was imminent. He loosened the bow from his shoulder and poised his spear, ready to hurl it if anything dangerous appeared.

Suddenly he stopped. From the dense undergrowth immediately before him, he could hear the bushes and bracken being forced apart. They burst open and an animal, huge, with a woolly coat and a horn atop its head, came galloping towards him, roaring like an incensed bull. It had its head lowered, aiming the point of its horn at Ezon as it charged him. Ezon hurled his spear hard and sharp into the exposed neck, just behind the beast's lowered head. The beast's momentum slowed somewhat. Ezon strung an arrow to his bow, and no sooner had one arrow found its mark than another was on its way. The animal came to a slithering halt, its legs buckling underneath; it capsized in a heap, the glaze of death in its eyes.

Everything happened so quickly that Moorgate and Atholle were only beginning to feel the terror of it when it was all over.

Ezon walked over to the slain beast and reclaimed his spear and arrows, unruffled, as if nothing had happened. His sleight of speed with the weapons had been almost as frightening as the charging animal. Then the beast shrivelled before their eyes, the carcass simply disintegrating into nothingness. But the ground where it had fallen was not completely bare; a conch shell lay there. Ezon picked it up.

'It must have a purpose,' he thought.

'Blow it,' said Atholle.

'No, not here.'

Ezon handed the conch to Atholle and they walked in silence across the plain towards the peaks of the Flante.

The mountains were solid and dark, and the peaks reached almost to the verge of the clouds. When they reached the lower slopes of the mountains, three solid rock towers, about a hundred yards apart, stood before them. They were windowless, except for a solitary slit set high in the throat of each tower. The first tower was higher than the second, and the second higher than the third. The tops sloped downwards into the nearest mountain.

Ezon halted, and consulted the map. He paced to within sixty yards of the first tower. The sun was at his back. He asked Atholle for the conch, put it to his lips and blew a long roaring blast on it. It had the roar of an animal. The ground quaked in front of them, and although it was hard with a mixture of clay and rock, hoof-marks formed. The clay and rock loosened, a small circle of ground burst open and a black marble pillar rose about thirty feet above the nearest tower. The sunlight glanced off the top of the pillar and sent a dazzling beam of light through the slits in the towers and into the face of the mountain. Ezon threw the conch into the hole the pillar had burst through. The earth stopped quaking and they moved up the mountain to where the sunlight shone off the rock-face.

Not long after the old woman who had watched them in Malstorn struggled up the mountain in their tracks.

As they reached the place where the sloping beam of light struck the face of the mountain, the bare rock opened before them and they walked in. There were passageways going right and left and centre. Ezon checked the map in the gloom, then they walked forward, down a wide tunnel, until they came to a huge cavern. It was full of creatures — creatures who had eyes made of diamonds and teeth which seemed to be made of silver. Their arms were red and white, as were their faces and legs. Their hair was braided, and their nails were long and bronze-coloured. They talked and laughed and laughed and growled. Some spat silver sparks; others spluttered smoke. And they were all armed with clubs of stone and rusty tin. They were rock-creatures.

Ezon pointed his spear at them.

'Strike us with any weapon and the mountain will come

down about your heads!' belched one of the creatures.

'And about your head too!' roared Ezon back. 'Better the mountain comes down upon us than the humiliation of your freakish clubs!'

'Freakish!' screeched the creature. 'There is nothing freakish about our clubs!'

'Maybe not,' retorted Ezon insolently. 'But there is certainly something freakish about yourselves.'

'Speak for yourself,' laughed the creature, 'and your companions. Look, one is no bigger than a hiccup, and the other wears clothes as if they were strangling him.'

The creature who had spoken was not the only one who laughed. They all laughed, and blue smoke came out of their ears. They all spat sparks, and some of their eyes began to glow. And as they laughed their ears flapped and their streaky black hair tossed as if in the wind.

'We don't wish to harm you,' said Ezon, 'but if harm is what you want then harm is what you will get.'

'I said, if you harm us the mountain will come down about your heads!'

'And yours too!' retorted Ezon.

'Wrong! Wrong! That's where you're wrong! We're part of the mountain. The mountain will not harm us. We are sons and daughters. Fathers and mothers. Grandfathers and grandmothers.'

'Great-grandfathers and great-grandmothers more likely,' snarled Ezon. 'But probably older than the mountain itself. You certainly look it.'

'Don't be so cheeky.'

'Does the truth hurt?'

'Not as much as the mountain.' At this the rock-creatures all laughed; they sounded as if tiny stones were grinding inside their mouths.

Ezon tried to push a way through the rock-creatures but they would not move. Some even jumped down off the cavern ledges. They flashed sparks and snorted puffs of smoke, and never stopped, not until their leader told them to. He then turned to Ezon and said:

'Since you have passed the three giant towers of Autern you will be granted one wish. And whatever it is you wish for, each of you can only have one, while each of us will have two.'

'Can we wish for any one thing?' asked Moorgate.

'You can wish for anything, but only one wish. And whatever it is you get one each, while we get two.'

'It is called simple arithmetic,' laughed one of the lesser rock-creatures.

'Simple cunning,' put in another.

'Cunningly simple,' shouted a third.

'I will tell you what we will wish for,' said Moorgate. 'We wish to be blind in one eye.' He felt very pleased with himself for being so smart. His chest puffed and his cheeks reddened. He was really pleased with himself.

The rock-creature leader's face went purple with rage. In fact all the rock-creatures' faces went purple. They howled, and gradually their rage turned to howls of anguish as the sight faded from their eyes, and the walls of the cavern were no more, only blind darkness.

Ezon, Moorgate and Atholle, although they were blinded in one eye, did not care. They rushed past the rock-creatures and left them to fall over one another and stumble into the damp walls of the cavern and its auxiliary tunnels. They walked through four different passageways until they came to tunnels that were narrower than the ones belonging to the rock-creatures. For a while they were in total darkness until they came to some steps which led downwards. There was light from torches fixed in metal holders on the walls. They walked down the steps into a deep cavern scattered with the warm circular glow of camp-fires that gaped from the blackness of the cavern floor.

Groups of goblins sat around the camp-fires, chattering and toasting themselves, almost as if they were sunbathing on a fine summer's day. They wore no clothes, and were red all over. They all looked the same — ugly and awful. Some had pronged spears which they used to poke the fire. The fires were coal fires and the smoke plumed thickly up into the sooty roof of the cavern, and hung about in heavy cough-filled clouds which slowly filtered through black holes which were cave chimneys, and went through the mountain for nearly a mile and trickled into the light air that mantled the snow-clad peaks of the outer world.

When the goblins saw Ezon, Moorgate and Atholle coming down the steps into the cavern, they all stood up and hissed with long lizard-like tongues. Each and every last one of them roared. But Ezon, Moorgate and Atholle kept on coming towards them. One extra stout-hearted goblin threw a few burning coals at Ezon — but they fell short. The goblins began to feel crestfallen. They stopped hissing and roaring and throwing lumps of coal. One of their number stepped forward. He had what looked like a lump on his head, but it really was a crown, a precious goblin crown.

'I'm Azuire, king of the goblin fires,' he said. 'How did you get into the mountain?'

Ezon told him, and immediately Azuire took a dislike to him; he knew that Ezon was not afraid of him.

'Another question: How did you pass the rock-creatures?'

When Ezon told Azuire that the rock-creatures were blind and would remain so, some of the goblins quickly heated their pronged spears and dashed off up the steps to torture the unfortunate blinded rock-creatures.

'Your fires give great heat,' said Ezon.

'They do,' conceded Azuire, 'but not as much as the furnaces of the Bright Lights.'

'Bright Lights? Who are they?'

'They stoke gigantic furnaces. They're so diligent that

anything they see is thrown into the furnaces.' Azuire gave a hoarse laugh. 'They're what you call singularly single-minded.' He ceased his guffawing. 'They're made of flames and we can't attack them because the flames make us feel itchy all over.'

'Can we sit at your fire for a while?'

'Sit at it? You can sit *in* it.' The hoarse laugh erupted again.

Ezon sat at the fire. So did Moorgate and Atholle; the tunnels had been damp and they were glad of some heat. Neither of them spoke to the goblins although questions were asked and insults conveyed. Moorgate was too proud to converse with such uncouth creatures. Atholle was too afraid.

Some of the goblins took Atholle's wine pouch from him and quickly got drunk. 'More! More!' they shouted, and more, more they drank until they began to belly-ache.

Atholle snatched the pouch back from them.

'I want to give you a present,' Ezon said to Azuire. 'I want to give you all a present.'

'What kind of present? A stupid present?'

'No, a good one. One which will protect you from the itch of the Bright Lights.'

'That we'll accept. Give it to us.'

'This sword I have is enchanted.'

'So what? Just give us the present.'

'The present has to be given by the power of the sword.'

'You mean, chop our heads off?' hissed Azuire.

'No. Have you heard of Morthern?'

'Morthern the blacksmith? Morthern of Hasutti? Yes, I have heard of Morthern.'

'This sword was given to me by Morthern. I can draw a flame from it. A flame which will always protect you from the itch of the furnaces and the Bright Lights.'

'How? How will it work, this flame?'

'I will draw it from the camp-fire, and let it rest above your head. It will follow you everywhere, and if you are threatened it will expand and engulf your attacker in flame. It will protect you and counteract the itch from the furnaces and the Bright Lights.'

'Lovely! Give me this flame until I burn the Bright Lights with it. And I want mine bigger than the others ... much bigger ... !'

Ezon smiled and said he would only be too happy to confer Azuire and his followers with a flame. The goblins were all delighted. But one of the lesser goblins complained. 'What about my brothers and the others who went up the tunnel to the rock-creatures?'

'What about them?'

'They won't get a flame.'

'That's their problem.'

'But that's not fair.'

'Who wants to be fair? Life wouldn't be worth living if everything was fair.'

'My brothers won't like it if they don't get a flame.'

'My brothers won't like it either, and they're bigger than me, and you know what that'll cause. There'll be family rows. Sons will beat up fathers, and fathers will beat up grandfathers. Daughters won't talk to mothers, and mothers won't talk to anyone. We can't have that.'

'Why not?'

'It'd make life rotten.'

'It'd be bad for the rule of law and order.'

'I hate law and order!'

'So do I.'

'We all hate law and order!'

'I don't!'

'That's only because you're small and weak. You ought to be ashamed of yourself.'

'I would like to speak.'

'Shut up!'

'Yes, shut up! You haven't opened your mouth in three

years except to hiss and spit.'

'That's a lie!'

'It's a truthful lie. You're only a hisser and a spitter, and something else that sounds like a hisser, but isn't.'

'Stop this! Stop this nonsense!' Azuire called the goblins to order. He hissed and glared, and prodded some of the more rebellious with a white-hot fork, before making them all line up in a queue in preparation for the magnificent gift which Ezon was about to bestow. He wanted to be the last to accept the flame, but he would not get into the queue. Instead he stood next to Ezon, as if he was overseeing the mysterious flame that was being bestowed on them as they knelt before him. Ezon had taken the flame from the camp-fires, letting Morthern's sword soak in the red coals; he then crossed the blade above the goblins' lowered heads so that the flame would float there for — for, who knows how long?

When it came to Azuire's turn the whole cavern was hushed and still. The goblins could hardly believe their eyes when he knelt before Ezon. He was little known for being humble and it came as a great surprise to them to see him kneel. They even noticed him look up to make sure his flame was bigger than the others. As soon as Ezon had crossed the blade above his head, all the goblins' flames began to itch, including Azuire's; only his itched more, because his flame was bigger.

Ezon, Moorgate and Atholle did not wait to see how long the itch would last. They rushed past the goblins and stood in the far corner of the cavern, checking the map to see which of the many tunnels would bring them to the furnace-home of the Bright Lights. The goblins were too busy scratching their black-veined bodies to pay any heed. It took a few minutes to figure out which tunnel was the correct route to take, and as soon as they had found the right one they were gone from the scratch-crazed goblins.

Back in the cavern, the goblins' itch became unbearably unpleasant. Azuire got into a dark hole and scratched away.

He did not want the other goblins to see his predicament for
fear he would be belittled in their eyes, and a new king of
goblins elected in his place. But hiding was impossible; he
was dragged from the hole by some of the goblins who had
gone up the tunnels after the rock-creatures. His reign as king
was finished. They took the crown from his head and threw
him back into the hole.

A new king was elected from one of those who had escaped
Ezon's trickery with the flame. He made a speech: 'We'll all
go after this sorceror and his two supporters. We will use white-
hot prongs, fire, goblin evil, mad eyes, and disordered lunacy.
We'll go through the mountain and help the Bright Lights,
because the rock-creatures were tricked, we were tricked, and
the Bright Lights will be tricked. We'll all unite and defeat
the sorcerer and his two henchmen. Follow me!'

But the new king was not really able to lead. He had not
been born a king. He was only an ordinary goblin and the
other goblins had no respect for him. Azuire was the only
one who had been born a king. But now, he too had lost their
respect. The goblins declared the election null and void. They
would never have a king again, not as long as the itching lasted,
and then, Azuire would have to be reinstated. But, for the
moment, those who had come back from tormenting the rock-
creatures rushed after Ezon and the others. But they did not
get very far. Some of the flames came after them and they
too became itchy, so they rushed back to their own cavern
where the flames were transferred again to their rightful owners.
From that moment on the goblins never left their own cavern,
not even to go and torment the rock-creatures.

When Ezon, Moorgate and Atholle got to the underground
domain of the Bright Lights they were amazed. The Bright
Lights had no heads, arms or feet. They were ever-changing
shapes of twisting flame. Even so, they constituted no danger
to the three intruders. Their sole purpose seemed to be to
feed the furnaces which were built, in pockets, into the walls

of the cavern. They were fed lava which poured along rock drains from ducts, and was sluiced into the furnaces by the Bright Lights, who really were nothing better than bondaged slaves.

When they left the domain of the Bright Lights, Ezon checked the map again. Then they entered a wide tunnel; a silver light began to filter through, and they followed it until they emerged.

They were standing on the slope of a mountain. In the sky above, there were three moons and a silver rainbow. Rain seemed to fall down out of the moons and drift in squalls across the curve of the rainbow. But it was only an illusion, because the ground was dry. Moorgate heard the sound of running water from a mountain stream nearby. He led the others to it and they washed in the stream. When they finished washing they realized that their partial blindness was gone.

'I hope, said Moorgate, 'that the rock-creatures have got their sight back too.'

'Well, ours came back,' said Ezon. 'Maybe it will take a little longer. They were greedy.'

'None so blind as those who will not see,' said Atholle, which was about the wisest thing he ever said. Or ever would.

They checked the map again and walked down into the valley of the Flante.

The old woman who had been in Malstorn had come through the mountain after them. She beckoned to them but Ezon would have nothing to do with her. He feared she was a sorceress and told the others to quicken their pace, so as to get away from her.

The old woman was tired and she sank to the ground as Ezon walked away into the distance.

After a while a shadow formed on the stalky tufts of mountain grass where she rested. It was a human shadow with a side profile. Then the shadow turned towards her, the arms opened wide and the dark outline of a cowl showed. The old woman could see a face. It was that of Nadair! She winced and moved her hand hesitantly towards it, but as she did it weakened and disappeared.

The old woman was glad it had gone. She was scared but all the more determined to meet up with Ezon in the hope that he would help her in her hour of need.

17. Knights without Armour

It took Ezon, Moorgate and Atholle nearly four hours to climb down the mountain to the floor of the valley, and before they had reached the bottom, the sun had risen. Mountain peaks flanked the long funnel of the valley, shuttering out the horizon from the shaded valley floor.

Atholle was fed up. He wanted to sit down and drink from the wine pouch, and Moorgate would have given anything for a puff of tobacco and a daydream. But Ezon was determined to press on, even though it was hard for Moorgate to keep up and Atholle's feet ached with tiredness; he had never walked so far in his entire life and the thought that they would have to tramp every last inch of the valley's humpy ground made him miserable.

In the end Moorgate rebelled and refused to walk any further without taking a rest and smoking a pipeful of tobacco. Ezon realized he was being a little too hard, especially on poor Moorgate, so he said nothing, and Atholle plopped down beside the jaded elf and had a few draughts of wine, moaning about how tired he was and how he should have never left the island on such a dangerous adventure. Moorgate had taken his pipe and pouchful of tobacco and was packing a shredded leaf of tobacco into the bowl of the pipe when he looked up. Instinctively, he knew the sun was behaving abnormally; it was not arcing from East to West; it was moving from South to North.

'The sun is going from South to North,' he said. Ezon just looked at him and shrugged in disbelief. 'When the compass won't hold there's no way of knowing.' And in truth, as Ezon held the compass the needle spun madly, making it impossible to read.

'Take out the map,' said Moorgate.

But the map was blurred and illegible.

The ground began to rumble and the sun spun madly in the sky. Moorgate's pipe fell from his hand and wedged between some rocks. Then, just as suddenly, the rumbling stopped and the sun settled. A scrawny vulture swooped from the sky. Ezon slug an arrow to the taut string of his bow and let the arrow thud into the vulture's underbelly. It plummeted to the ground — but it did not lie down! It turned into Nadair and lunged at Ezon. But Ezon sidestepped and drew Morthern's sword. When the wizard saw the steel of the sword he vanished in a puff of smoke. Moorgate had fallen down into a crevice between the rocks where his pipe lay and Ezon had to pull him out. The little elf had the pipe clutched in his hand.

'He will be back,' muttered Moorgate in embarrassment. 'Next time I will be ready.' He was furious with himself for having fallen among the rocks. But at least he had got his pipe back. He would not have to go to the bother of whittling another one.

'All this is too dangerous,' whined Atholle. 'Let someone else take care of it. Why can't we go home?'

Ezon was furious with Atholle. 'If we lived in trees, like you, perhaps we would have been too cowardly to get involved in this quest.'

'I am not cowardly. I only live in trees to keep out of danger.'

'There's plenty of danger now. Why don't you go and climb a tree?'

Moorgate did not like what Ezon said. Atholle pretended he had not heard the remark, but his pride was hurt.

Just then, a shadow passed over the sun. Its darkness touched

off Ezon and Atholle — but it did not affect Moorgate, because
he would not allow it to. He knew exactly what the shadow
signified but he did not bother to explain the facts to the others.
Nadair was trying to use his wizard's magic to weaken their
resolve. But Moorgate had enough elf powers to ward off the
evil shadow. Ezon or Atholle were unaware that anything was
happening, except that the shadow melted, and the mountain
slopes and valley glittered in warm sunshine.

'Look at the map again,' instructed Moorgate. This time
the outlined features were firmly fixed, as was the compass.
But more significantly, the sun had changed position in the
sky. It arced from East to West, its true trajectory.

Ezon noticed something moving in the distance. As it came
closer the blurred objects turned into galloping horses. There
were six in all. Three were riderless, one of them much smaller
than the others, smaller even than a pony. Charbonne, Patti
and Simon were on the others. They had passed through the
dream-world and reached the valley safely. Charbonne was
mounted on a chestnut pony, while the others rode grey
geldings.

Moorgate waved a polka-dot handkerchief to attract their
attention. But he need not have worried; Charbonne knew
exactly where they were. He led the way up the slope to where
Moorgate and the others stood, the three riderless horses close
behind on a long lease of reins that streamed from Charbonne's
grip.

Ezon was amazed at how well Charbonne could handle the
pony and the trailing horses. At that instant he looked much
more commanding than a child. He undid the reins of the
spare horses from his grip and told Ezon and the others to
mount up as there was much to be done, and that it should
be done sooner rather than later.

Moorgate, of course, mounted the smaller-than-small pony.
Surprisingly, Atholle got the best of the other two horses
because Ezon was busy looking after the bundle containing

the crown and sword. Charbonne said they were to follow him, as he knew what was to be done, and how. He mentioned a rock in the shape of an old woman's head, and said that Ezon was to hand him the compass at the rock, and the map was to be buried there.

'Who told you all this?' asked Ezon.

'Gadua,' retorted Charbonne in a child-like lilt.

Without saying any more he led the way through the wild grass flatlands until they came to the rock which was in the shape of an old woman's head. Ezon handed over both the map and the compass. He scooped a shallow hole with Morthern's sword, and Charbonne placed the folded map in the hollow of the hole, and buried it with loose clay. They stood for a while looking at the rock. It looked uncannily life-like, and the longer they stared at it the more real it became.

'Let's leave here,' Ezon said. 'I don't want any dealings with old hags or wizards. We've enough to do without being burdened by bad luck.'

They left the rock and rode in a line beyond a bend in the valley where a lone horseman could be seen riding towards them. As the rider came closer they could see he was a knight of sorts. Ezon readied his spear, but he quickly lowered it when he saw the drab rusty armour the knight was clad in. He cut a sad spectacle. He was slumped forward as if wounded. But when he opened his vizor to speak they realized he was not wounded but deeply dejected.

'Pray, I ask you, have mercy on a poor unfortunate knight.'

'And why should we have mercy?' asked Ezon.

'Such has been my bad luck, and the luck of my comrades, I doubt if there is any such commodity left in the whole cruel world.'

'Well, you can have mercy here once you are not a threat,' said Ezon, appalled at the delapidated state of the knight's armour. 'Where is your shield and your coat of arms?'

'Both gone. Buckled into a white heat and melted.'

'How could that be so?' asked Ezon, almost in disbelief, but attempting to conceal his contempt for the wretched knight.

Patti and Simon felt like offering their sympathy too but they were afraid to say anything in case Ezon would despise them. It was obvious that the poor knight was down on his luck, and all he wanted was a kind word.

'How could anything not be so,' bemoaned the knight, 'when I and my band of fine knights were set upon by a powerful wizard?'

'Wizard? Who might he be?'

'Nadair. Four of my knights recognized him instantly. But in that instant he was upon us and confounded us with his magic. Look!'

So saying, he drew his sword from its scabbard. Charbonne and Atholle laughed at the sight. Once clear of the scabbard it flopped to one side and wobbled like a piece of weak rubber.

'He did this. He rusted our armour and melted our shields and insignia. He even made two of our horses talk. All they do is shout insults and abominations.'

'How many knights are there?'

'Fourteen. But they are too heavy-hearted, and utterly confused. You see, the wizard committed one other atrocity. He blanked our minds and we cannot remember where we came from, or the purpose of our quest. We cannot remember a dot, except we are lost fools of the world, to be laughed at and ridiculed.'

'We won't laugh at you, Sir Knight,' vowed Ezon. He looked to the others, and they all nodded approval.

'Yes, "Sir Knight", it will have to be,' moaned the knight. 'I can't even remember my name. "Sir Knight" will be as good a name as I will ever have again.'

'No, you will have your own name.'

'How can I, when it's lost to my memory?'

'Bring us to your comrades. Our elf friend here has powers which can cure wizards' maladies.'

'I don't see how an elf can help.'

'He is no ordinary elf. Trust in him and he will not fail you or your fellow knights.'

The cavalcade of seven horses and riders rode on until they came to the place where the knight's fourteen companions sat in a dazed state, shocked by the humiliating misfortune which was their lot. Their horses were there too, tense and frightened, prancing nervously, hocks and leg muscles flexing fitfully. Some foamed at the mouth, and — as the knight had said — two of them were able to talk. Moorgate was startled. Their voices sounded distinctly like Nadair's. He told Ezon so, but he thought it of little interest; all he wanted was that Moorgate should cure the unfortunate knights and their horses.

Moorgate saw to the horses first. Ezon lifted him up on to each one and he craned forward to spread his hands on the horses' foreheads. They calmed down and became docile, succumbing easily to his touch. But not the two horses which ranted insults and obscenities. They could not be caught at all, until Charbonne approached them; then they calmed immediately. Moorgate pressed the palms of his hands to their foreheads. The horses uttered one or two oaths and then broke into a vicious jibberish. But the louder the jibberish became, the stronger Moorgate became. A red haze built up around him. The horses' speech became distorted and Moorgate moved his hands on to their throats. They began to neigh and Moorgate knew the wizard's spell was broken. The red haze evaporated, gone as smoke on the wind.

Next, Moorgate turned his attention to the knights. He got Patti and Simon to gather their melted shields and place them in a circle around the knights. He told Ezon and Atholle to take the knights' rubbery swords, scoop out some clay from the ground and place the swords in the holes. Then Moorgate seemed to go into a trance. The red haze built up around him again. But it did not stay there. It broke into long rapier-like slivers and struck off the shields, and from there the haze

extended into the full blades of the swords, and on to the
knights' rusty armour.

During all this time Moorgate walked around the outside
of the circle, halting briefly at each shield, and pointing his
finger as if in accusation. But he did not speak; he did not
incant; he did not accuse. When he came to the last shield
and pointed, the red slivers came together and drifted until
they hovered around Moorgate and quickly dissolved. The
knights were their former selves again; they were no longer
in a state of shock and their memories were restored. The
formerly rusty patchiness of their armour was bright and shiny,
the emblems of their knighthood emblazoned between the
massive curves of the shields. Their swords were straight and
strong and were steel to the touch. The knights were glad
to be rid of their cursed afflictions. Each one of them shook
Moorgate's hand in gratitude, and although Moorgate did not
show it, he was deeply touched by their consideration.

The knight whom they had first met explained, 'We are
lord knights who serve the cause of justice. And we deemed
the missing children from the East to be worthy of such justice.
We were on a quest to rescue them when Nadair came in
the form of a raven and put a curse on us.'

Ezon was puzzled, as was Moorgate. How had they been
able to bring their horses through the dark underground mesh
of tunnels and the chambers of the rock-people? The horses
would have bolted in terror. They would not have been able
to manoeuvre the clefts and ledges that riddled the inside of
the mountains.

But the knights explained that they had not entered the
valley by way of the tunnels. They had come in from the
North, a long trek that had taken weeks, and had encountered
a lot of trouble from greedy mountain bandits who infested
the route.

When they had finished their story, Ezon suggested that
they join forces to free the missing children. The knights readily

agreed to be part of the alliance. It put added fervour into all their hearts and almost made Atholle feel brave.

But surrounded by fighting men with heavy swords and lances, and armour that brightly reflected the crouched dazzle of the sun as it broke through the clouds, with the noise of horses' hooves sounding like a drumbeat, Patti and Simon felt uneasy. It was almost as if they were going into battle, the closed visors and the vivid emblems of the knights' insignia a fair warning that mortal combat could be triggered off at any moment.

Before long, they came to a castle. Not the castle where the seed was to be sown but a heavily guarded fortress which protected the outer regions of Nadair's domain.

Charbonne had them rein in. He knew of the castle, and of the champion knight who challenged all comers. Nadair would be there too, disguised as a fire-dragon, just as the Subservients had prophesized. Ezon would have to challenge both if they were to continue on their quest to free the children.

Ezon walked forward in full view of the sentries who stood on the ramparts. He shouted up and asked that the captain be sent for. When the captain came he scowled and asked Ezon what he wanted.

'You champion knight's head!' retorted Ezon.

'From where you stand, haughty one, my archers could cut you down, and no further ado. But since you want our champion's head I think it better game to let him avail of yours. No doubt you would rather die at the sword of a noble knight than by a common archer's arrows. Such is the dullness of your person, no doubt your swordmanship is equally as dull!'

'Captain, send me this knight so that he can feel the dullness of my blade.'

'You can have him by and by. Tell me, what is the motive of your quest, apart from challenging the good knight?'

'To prove my prowess, and then to claim the head of the

dragon you hold in the castle dungeon.'

'Claim the dragon's head!' laughed the captain, as did those on guard. 'There is only one way to claim the dragon's head, and that is by smiting it in combat.'

'That,' said Ezon, 'is what I want. To take the dragon's head in combat.'

'Stranger, I despise you. Surely you must be wanton to wish such. I will have to reject your challenge. My knights are not given to slaying madmen.'

'I am not mad! Send me your champion until I prove my prowess.'

'No! Rather I would have you slain in a hail of arrows, for you are no better than a mad dog.'

'Sir,' said Ezon. 'Amongst these lofty mountains there must be eagles. In the loneliness of your day I would say you have captured a few to while away the long hours of boredom.'

'Eagles there are,' retorted the captain, 'but not for the purpose of your amusement.'

'What purpose then? To snatch away babies from peasants?'

'You tongue, stranger, is without wit.'

'Wit or without, I am true to my word. A pigeon, then, can you not spare a pigeon? Surely you have such for sending messages, as I am told your men are afraid to carry messages from the castle for fear they might lose them.'

'To temper your insults we will throw you a hawk.'

'Good, let me have it.'

'And may it tear the eyes from his head,' muttered the captain, his men alone hearing what he had said.

A hawk was brought and the captain nestled it on his gloved hand, saying, 'Go to him, tear. For he is no more than a rabbit.' He released the hawk, and it rose high in the sky, readying itself to swoop on Ezon.

Ezon put an arrow to his bow and trained it on the hovering hawk. It finished hovering and swooped down in a quick defiant flight, claws out-stretched and eager to make impact.

Ezon drew on the bow, the hawk in its swoop having already cut the distance by half. The distance was shortly halved again, as the arrow from Ezon's bow tore into the hawk's scrawny flesh. It plunged to the ground only feet away from Ezon.

'Your hawk is suffering from fatigue,' shouted Ezon to the captain. 'Pray send out the precious knight.'

Ezon had no sooner spoken than his words were drowned by the heavy grating of the main castle gate being opened. The figure of a mounted knight in armour came forward, sword in hand.

'Well, mighty warrior,' taunted Ezon, 'what is that in your hand, a candle? Come, I will light it for you.'

The knight sheathed his sword and came forward at a canter, his sword hand holding an iron ball, which had sharp spikes projecting from it, on a chain. He twirled the ball, and chain above his head, before lowering it to accomplish the slaying of Ezon. Ezon stumbled out of the way as the knight bore down on him, the momentum of his horse carrying him several yards beyond the spot where Ezon had been standing. He turned and charged again, but this time was a little too quick in passing. Next time, he was determined he would wheel in beside Ezon, pressing his horse closer so as to be able to strike more successfully.

But there was not to be a next time. As the horse passed Ezon he touched the strapping on its underbelly with his sword, and as the horse made its turn its mail cut through, dislodging both saddle and rider.

'Better learn to walk first,' said Ezon, a soft smile on his face, but steel in his eyes.

'Be done with your deed,' panted the knight, Ezon's sword at his throat, the flat of his boot on the knight's stomach.

'I have taken to dragons' heads,' hissed Ezon. 'Yours is an ugly head, but it is still not the head of a dragon.'

So saying, he slit the knight's armour with a firm but slight touch of the sword. 'Begone, and send out the dragon.'

'I would rather die than live with shame,' spoke the knight. 'Why don't you smite my head?'

'Begone!' retorted Ezon, taking the sword from the knight's scabbard for fear he would make a fight. 'Get to the castle, for I want not of mortal men.'

He watched as the knight made his way in disgrace back to the castle.

'Captain, it is easy to see why you command this hovel in the mountains,' shouted Ezon. 'I do not think you know who I am.'

'Some trickster suffering from a madness,' roared the captain in rage and hate. 'You will be much remembered for your cheekiness. For your end is nigh.'

A roaring noise erupted from behind the castle wall. The drawbridge dropped with a ringing thud and a dragon rushed out across the riveted beams. Ezon held Morthern's sword at the ready. The dragon charged and snorted dragon-fire, but the grim rapiers of flame were drawn into Morthern's sword. Above on the battlements archers had drawn up in a line. They had seen the knights in formation behind Ezon and they were prepared in case of an attack. Ezon pointed the sword at the dragon and unleased a searing blast of red flames. The flames spurted along the dragon's scaly back; it burst into a gigantic fireball of red and orange — and Nadair, in the form of a black raven, flew out of the inferno and off into the sky. Moorgate gave the signal for the knights to storm the castle, and as he did so Ezon spurted the remaining flame in the sword on to the battlements to keep the archers from obstructing the advance of the knights as they charged into the castle yard.

The fighting did not last long, and as the battlements were made of stone the castle did not catch fire. But the stone masonry on the upper walls glowed red and a sizzling sound could be heard. The captain and his men were all taken prisoner and locked up in the dungeons. Atholle wanted the keys thrown away but Ezon would not agree, and the knights said they would detail three of their number to look after the prisoners until someone could be found locally to see to the task.

Patti and Simon were the last to enter the castle, and just as they did, Charbonne gave a shout to look up into the sky. The children felt a giddy gladness seep into their hearts. Two horses had flown from the invisible depths of the horizon and were fast approaching the castle. Toria and Panri were on the horses, with Fraiter, and they guided the black and white steeds down to the green valley floor, hovering to wave before landing in the castle yard below.

Fraiter had a surprise for Atholle — he had the three buried food pouches with him. On Morthern's advice they had consulted Gadua. He had looked up one of his parchments, told Fraiter where they were buried, and advised him to bring them on the journey as the missing children would be in need of them. This Fraiter had done, and Atholle was overwhelmed with delight.

18. The Tree of Death

The children stole away to a private part of the castle. They had much to discuss. But first, the fabulous flying horses were fed and groomed. Patti especially was delighted to see them again. Only when all the chores with the horses were finished, did they relax and talk about the good, and not so good times, they had experienced since they last met.

The others kept to the main hall, where they feasted from Atholle's magic food pouches and discussed in detail the plan to attack Nadair's castle stronghold.

At dawn the cavalcade left the castle and moved up through the valley. Patti and Simon travelled through the sky with Toria and Panri, the horses flying with a lazy rhythm ahead of the knights. Eventually, they came to Nadair's castle and

hovered over the grey battlements and black pennant flags which flew from three of the four corner-turrets. The fourth turret towered much higher than the others, so high in fact that it must have been dizzy to look down from. This tower had a domed glass roof, but they could not see through it. The castle seemed to be deserted; there was not a living person to be seen. But their hearts were chilled by the sight of a line of skeletons dangling from poles against the back boundary wall. They did not wait to see any more.

They flew on until they came to a canyon deep in the valley floor. The sides were pock-marked with caves, and first Patti and then Toria saw dragons peeping from the entrances. Then they saw, far down on the floor of the canyon, children in their thousands, backs bent as they tilled the harrowed ground. They were looking at the missing children of the East!

Nadair's guards stood over them, firm and gaunt. Some carried whips; others were archers. They wore no insignia except for combat dress of black mail.

The guards saw the sky-travellers coming. The children did too. But the horses came no closer; they wheeled in the sky and flew back the way they had come before the children in the fields had a chance to recognize them.

They journeyed back to where Ezon and the others were approaching Nadair's castle. They landed in front of the marching column, and Ezon was told of the seemingly deserted castle and the sighting of the missing children in the canyon.

Ezon felt triumphant.

'The canyon, can we enter it on horseback?'

Patti said they could, that it was very accessible.

Ezon was pleased and he motioned with his hand for the column to proceed on its march to within shouting distance of the castle's battlements.

Ezon and Moorgate entered the castle first. It seemed to be empty, so they signalled from the battlements for the others to approach. The knights took up position on the battlements and kept an eye on the castle's outer entrances in case of a surprise attack. All the others, except Moorgate and Ezon, went to the walled garden, where the seed which the Corvey gave Charbonne was to be planted. But they did not sow it straight away. They waited as Moorgate and Ezon searched through the castle for Nadair. They finally went into the glass-domed fourth turret. There in one of the rooms the charred cinders of a log fire smouldered in the grate and the remnants of a meal lay on a table.

'He is here,' muttered Ezon, quickly searching through the room. 'He ate on his own, and he can die on his own!'

'He is not here,' said Moorgate simply. 'Find his coven and you will find him.'

They searched the rest of the turret, but not until they came to the room directly beneath the glass dome did they find Nadair's retreat. Red and green lights filtered through the dome. 'Devil light,' said Moorgate. There was an altar, a wizard's circle, and a lighted candle as tall as a fully grown man. The walls were lined with mirrors.

Nadair appeared as if from nowhere; the mirrors throwing back his reflection a hundred fold. Ezon lunged Morthern's sword at the spot where the wizard had appeared but the blade merely smashed a mirror into jagged pieces. Nadair's image flashed from every mirror, and Ezon just did not know which one was real. He shouted out to Moorgate, 'Help me! I can't put an end to him!'

Moorgate felt strong and powerful, but in an angry sort of way. A glow-like haze built up around him. He shouted Nadair's name again and again, and when Nadair did not reply a roaring wind swept through the chamber. The mixed swirl of light was torn from the dome and it emptied from the chamber, along with the images of Nadair. But the mirrors quickly filled with his reflections again. Moorgate pointed at a mirror and a silver fireball shot out from the shield of haze and spurted in a diagonal from mirror to mirror, and as they shattered so too did Nadair's bodily presence disappear. They did not see him go. But both he and the wind were gone and the red haze subsided from Moorgate. He was tired and despondent. All he could say was, 'Nadair has gone into the garden. Go there. I will follow you in a second.' But in truth Moorgate had just seen a vision in the remnants of the red haze. Morthern's voice had spoken and told him that Nadair's life and death was in the seed which was to be sown in the castle garden.

Ezon looked back at Moorgate and said, 'But ... you must come now ...'

'Go and fetch the crown and sword. I will meet you in the garden.'

When Ezon got to the garden the others had already dug a hole for the seed. Ezon told them of what had happened in the chamber, and to expect Nadair to appear in the garden. But they waited for Moorgate to come from the turret before planting the seed.

It was not long before the little elf came into the garden. He mentioned the vision and what Morthern had said concerning the seed.

'Gadua told me it holds two lives,' said Charbonne, taking the locket of seed from his pocket and handing it to Moorgate.

'If it holds two lives how can it be the wizard's death knell?' queried Ezon.

'Death is not always an ending,' explained Moorgate bleakly. 'It is sometimes a progression.' He was full of the ways of Nature, and knew that Nature was always a progression, never an ending. 'I see you have picked the right place,' he said, looking at the hole. 'Though usually one place is as good as another.'

Fraiter asked him a question, but he did not get time to finish. A raven swooped from the castle walls and landed beside them. It changed shape and turned into Nadair.

'Keep away from here,' he hissed.

Patti and Simon looked at Nadair in total amazement. It was the first time they had ever seen the wizard. He looked exactly like Dresus.

'It's Dresus!' whispered Patti.

'Dresus is my brother,' ranted Nadair. 'We are twins!'

Nadair chuckled at how startled the children looked. He went over to the hole, looked into it and laughed again. But it was the last time he would ever laugh. Moorgate cupped the seed in his hand, and as Nadair looked into the hole Moorgate walked up behind him and threw the seed directly at the wizard's feet. The ground burst open and the withered trunk of a tree shot up and enveloped Nadair until he was part of the tree.

Ezon had to lift Moorgate up so that he could place the crown and the sword in the tree. But Moorgate did not resent this. He really was very humble and a down-to-earth type of elf.

Moorgate then told Patti and Simon, as well as Ezon, to rub the rings they had once been given in the shrine of the Ancients against the tree.

Something totally unexpected happened. The withered tree vanished and Nadair was standing there rooted to the spot. Right next to him stood Dresus, the crown on his head and the sword in a scabbard at his side. But he was not wearing the clothes of a king. Instead he wore the suit he had on when the yellow car had crashed into the pole. He had a glazed look about him. He was confused. He had been sitting in the day-room of the asylum eating from a bowl of porridge when, all of a sudden, he had the sensation of hurtling through the ceiling. He was not certain whether he was dreaming or not. He could see Nadair right there beside him, and all the others, and the two horses, and the knights on the battlements. And he had the crown and sword. But as soon as he touched the sword to make sure he wasn't dreaming he and Nadair vanished into thin air and the tree shot up again, only this time it had

four branches instead of two. Everyone, even Atholle, knew for certain that Dresus and Nadair were forever a part of the withered tree.

'I will never live in a tree again,' shuddered Atholle. 'You would never know who you were living with, would you?' He then drew Moorgate to one side and whispered: 'We'll be able to go back to the island soon. You'll come, won't you?'

'Yes.'

'Superb!' said a relieved Atholle. 'If you didn't I just don't know what I would do.'

'Morthern would look after you.'

'He wouldn't! He never does anything for me!'

Moorgate did not bother to answer. He walked back to the withered tree, away from Atholle. It was sad that Atholle had such a strong dislike of Morthern. After all, Morthern had helped tremendously throughout the quest for the missing children.

He scraped some bark from the tree with a penknife, and put it in a pocket of his elf-tunic. He knew he would have an important use for the bark later. It had been part of the vision in the shrine.

The knights had seen what had happened from the battlements. They came down and got their horses ready. The others left the garden, and together they all rode from the castle and headed for the canyon to free the children from their bondage.

Ezon and Fraiter led the column. The knights followed in a long glittering file, the glint of their armour dazzling in the sunshine. Charbonne was to the middle of the knights. Atholle and Moorgate brought up the rear.

The children waited a while and gave the small moving army a headstart before taking to the sky on the two flying horses. The girls shared the white horse; the boys the black stallion. First they came across Moorgate and Atholle who had fallen a long way behind the others. Moorgate shouted up to the

children to let him ride in the sky, so that he would get to
the canyon in good time to help to rescue the captured children.
It was not his fault that his pony was very small and could
not keep up with the rest. But the children would not listen.
They only waved good-bye and moved further ahead, and even
passed the host of knights. They brought the horses to ground
just short of the canyon, and waited for Ezon and the others
to catch up.

When the knights came to where the children were waiting
with the horses they did not halt for long, only long enough
for Ezon to issue a few short instructions before sweeping into
the canyon and engaging Nadair's guards in combat. Patti and
Simon, Toria and Panri, let them go on ahead. But just as
the knights were within sight of Nadair's guards the children
caught up and swept past them over the fields to where the
captive children were at work. Toria tore an embroidered
emblem of the East from his tunic and let it fall on to the
ground. Some of the children ran forward and picked it up.
They instantly recognized the badge as being the coat of arms
of the East. Any doubt as to the identity of the riders was
immediately dispelled, and the enslaved children downed tools
and began to walk back towards the stone huts where they
slept at night. In response, the guards began to whip them,
but the children replied by throwing stones.

Ezon and the others had ridden into sight. The guards turned
from the children and the archers formed block sections to
meet the onslaught of the mounted knights.

Ezon was magnificent in battle. He used sword, spear and
bow. Fraiter, too, did his bit, as did the knights, a due
compensation for the humiliation they had suffered at the hands
of Nadair. But Charbonne held back and kept to the fringes.
He detested violence, so he encouraged the children to stop
throwing stones; to go back to the huts and bolt themselves
in until the fighting was over.

By the time Moorgate and Atholle caught up most of the

fighting was over. The horses had landed and the children were comforting those children who had been whiplashed by the guards.

There was not much left of the guards. They were either dead or locked up in the stone huts. They had witnessed the power of Morthern's sword, and those who had survived had thrown their weapons away and surrendered. A dragon had ventured from one of the caves in the side of the canyon. It had snorted fire and Ezon defied it by raising Morthern's sword and blocking its progress. It spat flames, but Ezon warded off the flames by means of the sword and directed them back on to the dragon.

More dragons ambled stiffly from the caves and came down from the slopes of the canyon, incited by the burning mass of their comrade. They snorted fire and billowed red-hot flame from their fanged mouths, flames that multiplied so rapidly that Morthern's sword was unable to cope. But just as Ezon's life seemed lost, a green flame mixed with the others. It struck against an outcrop of rock, disintegrating it into tiny pieces before spurting over the heads of the other dragons, like green fire licking along a bone dry trestle.

'It is Celfy!' exclaimed the Royal Princess. 'It is our beloved dragon,' and she rushed, unafraid, between the flames of red and green. Celfy saw her coming and moved towards her. He stopped breathing his green flame and his eyes became placid and affectionate. The other dragons began to make their way back to the caves, their aggression checked by Celfy's presence. In truth, they were afraid of Celfy and his green flame.

'We have missed you so much, Celfy,' and with that Panri put her arms around his lowered head and kissed him on his scaly cheek. The Prince, too, had come forward and was completely overjoyed at seeing Celfy.

'We cannot thank you enough. Why must you live here amongst these horrid caves?' asked the Princess.

'Because,' said Ezon, 'this is his home and everything he

holds precious lives here.'

'But he loves us!'

'That may be true,' repeated Ezon, 'but everything he is lives here.'

'I want to see his home,' demanded the Princess. And although Celfy could not speak, he understood what she was saying and he led her, and the Prince, back to the cave which was his home.

'Will the dragon not harm them?' asked the knights.

'No,' explained Ezon. 'He was once their protector and always will be.'

With that he unleashed some of the flame from Morthern's sword on to the tilled valley ground. 'The guards, when they free themselves, can go elsewhere to sow seed. Search the huts, and if there is any food bring it here until I scorch it in the flame. Hunger enslaves, and it is time those guards felt its bite.'

Fraiter and the knights went to do as Ezon bid. Atholle clung to his magic food pouches all the more dearly. He did not want to suffer the awful helplessness of hunger. Nor did he want the pouches to be accidentally set alight. Not that that would have happened, but after all the excitement of the dragons and the battle with the guards, Atholle was feeling muddled and overawed. He was not too certain of what had happened, or what was about to happen next. So he hung on grimly to his pouches. They were all he had in the world. But the danger was all past; the guards were locked up, and the dragons gone back to the caves.

Eventually, the Prince and Princess, entered Celfy's cave world. It was immense and dark. But deep inside there was light and fire, and a cleft below which there was a deep pool. And there was a music-box on a rock. The Princess opened it, and all three, the Princess, Prince and Celfy, listened to the beautiful lilting tune. It brought tears to the children's eyes, and the dragon, too, felt sad. They had once owned the music-box, and it brought back memories of another time, another cave, when Celfy had provided for them with fire and light, and cared for them with the gentle aura of his goodly nature. They looked into his sad eyes, and the Prince and Princess talked to him, and although he could not answer back, they could sense invisible words in his eyes and they knew what he was thinking and how he felt. And they could feel love and gratitude for him, clad in his scaly skin with his wide-fanged dragon mouth. He was magnificent and gentle. He was uniquely Celfy, the only dragon of his kind in the Four Kingdoms of the World.

They spent an hour with him, and when they left he came to the mouth of the cave and looked sadly, but proudly, after them.

By the time they got back to the others, the tilled fields and food had all been scorched, and the dragon-fire emptied from Morthern's sword. Now Moorgate was the centre of attraction. He stood at the edge of the scorched fields, the heat of the dragon-fire still glowing from the singed clay, before the assembly of knights, Ezon and all the others. He stood firmly, the sting of smoke in his eyes, and scattered the powdered bark he had taken from the castle garden on to the harrowed but scorched soil. He said, 'In time a forest will grow here. And, as each tree in the forest will be separate, so will it weaken and isolate the powers of Dresus and Nadair, leaving them forever weak.'

The knights listened in wonder to Moorgate. They could not understand how a lowly elf could have powers of prophecy or destiny. But the others were not surprised, even Charbonne. He had often heard of the magic powers that Moorgate possessed, from Gadua, the old sailmaker.

'All you knights ...' continued Moorgate '... take your banners and stake them to the ground around the edges of where this great forest will some day grow. Let them be a reminder to the deeds you have carried out over these last few days, so that every traveller who passes by here knows of the people who succeeded in this quest.'

'I will stake Morthern's sword to the ground, too,' said Ezon. 'Now that the quest is completed I will have no further use for it, and it will be a tribute to his power.'

Moorgate did not answer Ezon. He really did not like making speeches, except when it was essential, like now. It was the first speech he had made in eight years, and the second most important speech of his life. He left the assembly and went and stood beside Atholle. Instead Charbonne answered Ezon.

'The sword has to be taken back to Morthern. He told me. And you are to bring Patti and Simon too. Morthern has something he wants to hand them personally. He has done everything to help and he has to be obeyed.'

'That's easily done, if Toria and Panri consent to give us the horses,' said Ezon diplomatically.

'Of course we do,' said the Princess.

'But we should be going home,' said Patti.

'You will. Morthern will direct you,' explained Charbonne.

'I thought the Ancients were the only ones who could do that?'

'They are, but Morthern can help too. And you don't need the horses to go to Morthern. You are to use the power of the rings you wear. It's much quicker that way.'

The speeches over, Charbonne, Fraiter, the knights, Atholle, Moorgate and the royal children gave food to the children from Atholle's bountiful food pouches. Ezon, Patti and Simon were about to use the rings, when they heard the noise of a commotion.

The old woman who had followed Ezon from Malstorn had arrived in the camp, and was arguing in a very distressed manner with Fraiter and Charbonne. Ezon, Patti and Simon went to see what was wrong. The old woman stared pitifully at Ezon. She had a sheet of white parchment folded in her hand.

'What's that you are carrying, old woman?' questioned Ezon,

pointing to the sheet she held in her hand. The old woman did not reply. Instead she handed him the parchment. He unfolded it and showed it to Patti and Simon. It was the exact map that Charbonne had buried beside the rock which had the peculiar image of the old woman engraved on it.

The image and the old woman were alike!

'Take the map to Morthern as proof of my plight,' lamented the old woman. 'Once I was a beautiful woman with three fine sons. I owned the castle that Nadair lived in, and most of the land in the Flante. But Nadair put a curse on me; he stole my lands and imprisoned my sons in the three towers of Autern. Tell Morthern I need his help to lift this curse of old age from my body, and to free my three sons from the towers. Tell him I took the map from the place where it was buried.'

With that the old woman broke down and sobbed, but Patti rushed forward to console her. As for Ezon, as he watched, he felt guilty for having earlier abandoned the old woman on the mountainside.

'And if I go back to the island,' interrupted Atholle, 'I want a palace built. After all, I am an associate of the Ancients.'

'Who told you that?' asked Ezon.

'The Subservients.'

The knights laughed.

'I am very important. If I go back to the island I must have a palace. I demand a palace!'

'You shall have what you want,' said Ezon impatiently.

'I shall? But when?'

'Whenever you shall.'

The knights laughed again.

Moorgate said nothing, but he and Charbonne knew that Atholle could have whatever he wanted once the Ancients consented to it.

By this time all the captive children had gathered around and they cheered and clapped as the knights staked their banners to the ground. Some even left their emblemed shields fenced to the scorched clay. They considered it a privilege to do so, as it would leave their names forever imprinted in the annals of legend. It certainly was not an opportunity to be missed.

It would take a long time to feed all the children, and Charbonne knew that in all probability (through using the rings) Ezon, Patti and Simon would be back from their visit to Morthern in Hasutti before the last child was fed. He looked away to his left, and there, in a hollow, a blinding flash shot skywards and he knew that Ezon, Patti and Simon, were already on their way to Morthern.

PART THREE

19. In Morthern's Kingdom

Ezon, Patti and Simon stood beneath a black undercleft at the entrance to a rock tunnel. Outside, the whole kingdom of Hasutti was full of ice and snow-filled glaciers. The harsh cold blasted off their faces and limbs. Although the mouth of the tunnel was sheeted in black rock with streaks of snow, inside the tunnel was bright and daylight seemed to wind from its circular eye.

They followed the tunnel until they came to an enormous underground cavern, with rock staircases and platforms that reached to the roof. Passages led from the platforms, and the light which came from them mixed with the main light which glowed like moonlight from the roof.

Ezon told the children to go up the steps and shout Morthern's name into some of the tunnels in the hope of finding him quickly.

As Morthern approached, Patti could hear his footsteps echoing through the tunnels. She called Ezon and by the time he got to the top Morthern was already out of the tunnel, his voice booming and beads of sweat glistening on his stoic-like face.

He shook Ezon and the children by the hand. 'I see you had that perpetual nuisance Atholle with you.'

'How did you know that?' asked Patti, almost at once wishing she had said nothing.

Morthern took one look at her and said, 'How do I know? Come, I will show you.' He turned and climbed the steps, and as they followed him Simon looked through a crevice into an adjoining cavern where there were tremendous furnaces that crackled with flames. There were troughs full of molten iron, countless blacksmith's tools, and a well full of water to cool metals in. And, of course, there were anvils, at least three.

Morthern brought them into a small chamber, barely big enough to hold six people. In one corner there was a short marble pillar, on top of which stood a white rock speckled with green.

'It's the stone!' said Patti.

'It is a similar stone, but not your stone!' corrected Morthern. 'What you are about to see will explain why I know so much about what has happened.'

A flow of water drained through a rock funnel beside the inside wall of the chamber. At one point it widened and formed a pool before trickling out through a hole in the end wall. As Morthern placed the stone in the pool and rested his hands on it, images began to form on the water. The children saw an ambulance speeding around a corner, a car crash into a steel pole, a man in a grey suit coming out of a phone box. Then the images faded; Morthern had taken his hands off the stone. But he had only paused for a second. He quickly replaced his hands on the stone. This time they saw Charbonne feeding the missing children of the East. Moorgate and Atholle could also be seen, as well as all the others.

Morthern took the stone from the pool and replaced it on the pillar. He made no reference to the images they had just seen. Instead, he said, 'I believe you have the map that the Ancients gave Atholle, and also a request from the woman whose cursed image is engraved on a rock. Hand me the map, but not here. At the furnaces. When the map is burnt the woman will be restored to her former beauty.'

When they got to the furnaces Morthern threw the map into the flames. He then asked Ezon to hand back the sword. Ezon looked downcast; the sword had created his fame and reputation, and served him well during his quest.

Morthern sensed what was going through Ezon's mind.

'You will have many future adventures,' he boomed. 'And for such there will be many different weapons. Come, I will show you.' He paused, and beckoned Ezon and the children to follow him, and with the sword in one hand and the scabbard hanging loose from the other he walked down some stone steps and into a torchlit corridor. 'We are going to the armoury where the weapons I make are kept. Ezon, you are favoured by the Ancients, and the availability of my weapons is proof of the Ancients' protection.'

They came to an iron door. Morthern opened the door and they were met by a sparkling light which splayed through a funnel in the roof and struck off a gigantic geode set into the floor. A purple light reflected from the stone penetrated into the furthest corners of the armoury. All about the walls hung weapons and all sorts of contraptions for all kinds of situations.

'The light from the geode protects the weapons. Anyone who enters and takes a weapon, except by my hand, will bear the full brunt of the weapons' sharpness.'

'You mean,' said Simon, 'a sword could fly off the wall all on its own and run me through?'

'Yes, and worse.'

'I couldn't think of much worse!'

'You have not lived long enough to see worse. Misdemeanours are always repaid, even if it takes a life-time.'

Morthern took a shield from the wall and handed it to Ezon. Immediately Ezon became invisible. Patti and Simon would have liked to have held the shield as well, but they were afraid to ask Morthern. He took the shield back and replaced it on the wall.

'Why don't *you* turn invisible when you hold the shield?' asked Patti. But he refused to answer; he simply ignored her question.

Morthern then showed Ezon an amulet. He explained that the wearer could be in three different places at the same time, as the amulet could create three images of the person who wore it. It was really quite simple. He wrapped it in a leather-type wallet, gave it to Ezon and told him to keep it safe inside his tunic, explaining that it would be needed to free the woman's sons from the towers at Autern: 'Those who are imprisoned in the towers have to be rescued by the same person and at the same time. Wear the amulet and the woman's sons will be freed.'

Morthern paused, and told Patti and Simon the reason he had asked them there. He wanted to give each of them an amulet similar to the one he had given Ezon. He knew of all the problems the children were having with scientists examining them, and more especially, having them followed, so he thought it a good idea to give them an amulet each, as it would confuse those who were following them, as well as having many other additional benefits. It would be as if they were three different people in one.

But Patti and Simon politely refused the offer. They said that the amulets would probably only get them into deeper trouble with the scientists.

'We'd much prefer,' said Patti, 'if you could do something about the time lapse — make it look as if we weren't gone at all.'

Morthern looked kindly at her and said, 'That has already been done. The Ancients have seen to it.'

Morthern then took them back to the cavern which was his main living quarters and gave them a substantial meal. When they had finished, he turned down all the lamps until only the bright flickerings from the furnaces shot against the cavern walls, and conjured shapes from the flames. The children enjoyed every minute of it. Outside the blue sky peered from its icy ledge, the snow and ice wrapped in a silver haze. But the children only felt the comfort of Morthern's hospitality.

Then they went back to the main cavern and up the tunnel, to where the snowy wastes mixed with the smooth screed of rock that was Morthern's underground world. There they stood until the rings they wore pulsed a red glow. In a quick explosion of light they were hurled back to the valley beneath the peaks of the Flante where all the others — including the old woman — awaited their return.

She was no longer old; she was young and beautiful! Ezon told her to mount up behind Patti, on Panri's magnificent white horse; Ezon, Charbonne and Simon rode Toria's black stallion. Together the two horses wheeled up into the sky and circled over the camp below, before setting off for the three towers where the woman's sons were held prisoners.

When they reached the towers, Charbonne gave Ezon the keys to the heavily locked tower doors. He had previously sent two of the Corvey, who had suddenly appeared when he was feeding the missing children, to Nadair's castle to search for the keys, and when they brought them back Charbonne told the Corvey to keep out of sight until the rescue of the three prisoners was completed.

Ezon put on the amulet and straight away he became three likenesses of himself. His bow and spear were also split into triple images, so each bodily image was equally well armed; a bow and spear to each. Patti and Simon were awe-struck at the change; Ezon was not. He strode about, all three of him, issuing instructions, and formulating a plan in case there would be hidden evil in the towers.

Patti, Simon and Charbonne each went to a tower with Ezon. The old woman — the beautiful woman as she now was — stood close by the horses and watched anxiously from a distance. The three groups approached the towers, keeping one another in sight, and waited until the last group was in position. Ezon flighted three flaming arrows, with long streamer-like strips of cloth, at the turrets. When the last one soared into the sky, the three groups rushed into the towers. Much to their surprise, they met with no resistance. The guards had fled; the towers were completely deserted.

Steps led up into locked lofts which were quickly opened. The woman's sons came forth — children no longer, they were now warriors. Their mother was delighted and could not thank the three Ezons enough. Ezon made it easier for her; he took off the amulet.

The woman and her three sons were ferried to the Flante on the horses, with Patti and Simon. One son took possession of the castle where Ezon had slain the dragon, another of the castle where Nadair had his shrine. The third son lived with his mother on the lands where the missing children of the East had sweated and toiled. In time he became a champion knight, renowned as the defender of the forest which Moorgate had planted from the bark of the withered tree. And although he never aspired to becoming a lord like his two brothers, he became more famous and was revered throughout Cromsutti.

When they got back to the camp the sun was low in the sky and Charbonne asked for hundreds of camp-fires to be built so that the children could sit around them and wait for the arrival of the Corvey. He went from fire to fire and sat and talked to the children. As he did so each fire rose from the ground and hung suspended in the darkness. Then numerous Corvey came out of the twilight fringes beneath the fires. They were mounted on phantom horses and had thousands of such spare horses with them, all looking like silver shadows, with sparkling jewels on the bridles and saddles. Charbonne told the children of the East to mount up. Toria and Panri were also to travel back to the East through the dream-world and let Patti and Simon ride the flying horses back to the East. Charbonne mounted too, and not a word was spoken by the Corvey, not as much as a hoof-beat heard, as the cavalcade moved off into the dream-world, back to the Kingdom of the East. The camp-fires hung eerily in the sky for the rest of the night, and only vanished the next day, early in the misty light.

The same day Ezon journeyed through the sky back to the East with Patti and Simon. Fraiter, Moorgate and Atholle travelled with the knights (not by way of the goblin caverns!) back along the route through the mountain passes and down

the narrow defiles on to the plains, until, eventually, they came
to Malstorn, where Captain Sikron was waiting to set sail for
the East.

Charbonne arrived in the East two days later, with Toria and
Panri. They had travelled with the Corvey and the rescued
children through the mysterious dream-world, first on
horseback, then across the Great Ocean in phantom ships.

When they arrived in the East it was the dead of night
and there was nobody about to see the ships anchor and unload
the children on the quayside.

Toria and Panri recognized the dock area immediately. The
other children knew where they were, too. They all cheered,
and the clamour of their voices stirred the citizens of the City
from their sleep, but not before the Corveys' phantom ships
had gone back to sea, Charbonne along with them. He did
not go directly to Gadua. Instead he travelled back through
the dream-world with two of the Corvey to the place where
he had buried the map beside the oddly marked boulder close
to the skyline of the Flante.

But, for the present, people were out on the streets, rejoicing
at the news that their children had been found, and soon the
harbour was aglow with lanterns. The City's bells rang out,
and those children who lived there were brought home
immediately. The remainder, with Toria and Panri were taken
to the Royal Palace, from where eventually the King's envoys
brought them to their homes in the country.

Everyone was overjoyed, not least the King and Queen, Azor
and Matoi.

Charbonne scraped at the ground where the map had been
buried. In its place were eleven gold coins — payment from
the Ancients for the rescue of the children of the East. He
turned each coin over. On one side was the image of a wizard,
on the other that of a withered tree. He put the coins in his

pocket and walked away from the rock into the dream-world, where the two Corvey whisked him back to Gadua with the compass, which had almost been forgotten in the delirium of adventure.

Gadua was glad to see Charbonne again. He made him sit down and tell him everything that had occurred. Then, when everything was recounted, he sat at his desk and wrote the whole adventure down. Later he went outside and stared at the river, a tributary of the very same river which had carried Moorgate and Atholle to the wizards' temple; the river at the mouth of which Captain Sikron had anchored the *Atcheze*. He turned away from it and went back into the house. The adventure had been somebody else's; but now that he had written it down the story was his, Gadua's.

It took a further six weeks for Fraiter, Moorgate and Atholle to arrive in the East on board the *Atcheze* with Captain Sikron. At first Atholle would not leave the ship, but his curiosity got the better of him and he visited the Royal Palace, solely to see if he could get any ideas for the type of palace he wanted for himself. But though intent on research, he would not attend any royal banquets or celebrations, and it was not long before he and Moorgate set sail for their island home on board one of Azor's ships, along with architects, builders and materials for the proposed palace which had become such an obsession with Atholle.

Travellers still came to the island to seek the Dial for the long journey to Morthern. But Atholle did not want to leave it any more, except to go to the island of the Ancients, and nobody would take him there. He was not too upset. He loved tramping around his palace, and shouting down the echoing corridors — he just loved echoes. He had a huge banqueting table built in case lots of visitors would come to the island. But no such thing happened, and he often ended lying on the table, surrounded by his magic food containers, crying himself to sleep. It made a good bed when he sulked and was too lazy to go upstairs to lie down.

Moorgate did not stay on the island all the time. Sometimes he went off on ships and had adventures. He even, on one occasion, visited his forest home.

Captain Sikron, although he did not play a significant part in the adventure, got a huge reward — which he squandered. But he made a quick return to Cromsutti where he undertook the journey to the castle garden where Dresus and Nadair were imprisoned inside the withered tree. He tried to burn it. Once in the past, because of greed, he had betrayed Dresus, and by putting the tree on fire he thought he would be free from any revenge that Dresus might inflict on him.

But the tree did not catch fire. Sikron regarded this as a bad omen, and when he got back to Malstorn and put to sea, a storm blew up and the *Atcheze* capsized. Over half the crew perished. Captain Sikron was among those who survived. He became a pale shadow of his former self. A broken and frightened man, he blamed his ill-luck on Dresus and Nadair. He had always been a very greedy and superstitious person, but it was superstition rather than greed which finally brought about his own downfall. And as the *Atcheze* sank down through the depths of the ocean, not only did a ship die; a legend also sank beneath the waves.

20. Royal Banquet

The horses flew in a direct line over the Great Ocean, and Patti and Simon felt relaxed as they looked down on the stillness of the sea. Ezon, too, was at ease, although he no longer had Morthern's sword. Hopefully, his destiny would lie in other directions, now that he had the amulet. Perhaps he should study his dead father's magical scrolls. Meridia could help him. But Ezon had no feel for wizardry in his blood. He was not akin to his father; he was a warrior by inclination.

It took three days to traverse the Great Ocean and the northern coastline of the East, but finally they came to the coastal landmarks which showed that their journey was almost at an end. First, they came to a coastal barrier dammed by gaping red rocks, inside which nestled a lagoon which teemed with wild-life. Past the lagoon they could see the profile of the low rolling hills to the north of the City: the City where Azor and Matoi had their palace, and where Toria and Panri would be waiting anxiously for their return. But Fraiter, Moorgate and Atholle would not be there. They were still travelling back from the Flante to meet up with Captain Sikron and the *Atcheze* for the two-week voyage to the East.

When the sky travellers came to the City they did not fly directly over it. Instead they came down in the countryside and cantered the horses into the City. Word soon went out that they had arrived. The streets were quickly lined with people who cheered all along the way, right up to the gates of the Royal Palace. As they went in through the gates the Palace guards formed a guard of honour, and banners and bunting bearing the royal coat of arms straddled the avenue as far as the steps of the Palace. Carriages were drawn up in front of the steps and royal stable-hands took the two sky horses to the stables to be fed and rested. Then there was a flurry of trumpets and Azor and Matoi walked out on to the main steps of the Palace, wearing royal crowns and costumes of brocade with gold trimmings. Toria and Panri stepped out after them, splendidly dressed in equal manner.

Ezon and the children were escorted up the steps by a royal guard. Ezon bowed. Patti made a dainty curtsey. Simon bowed with a sweep of his arm. The King and Queen were delighted to see them, especially Patti and Simon. They exchanged pleasantries, and then the King said the coaches were to parade through the City so that the people could pay homage and show their appreciation for the bravery of the daring group in bringing all the children safely home. Patti just wished that Moorgate and Atholle, and maybe Charbonne, could have been there to share in all the glory.

And she spoke her mind. 'One thing, Your Majesty,' she said to the King. 'You'll have to do the same for Moorgate and Atholle when they come.'

'And don't forget Fraiter,' added Simon.

'Nobody will be forgotten,' said the King. But Ezon pointed out that Moorgate would be too embarrassed to take part in a parade; as for Atholle, he would be better kept out of the public eye in case he would be laughed at.

They got into the gilded carriages and with a ceremony and pageantry that was awe-inspiring, they paraded through the City. The ordinary townspeople waved and cheered, and everybody was happy. When they got back to the Palace there was a banquet in honour of Ezon, Patti and Simon.

The banquet-hall was enormous, with row upon row of tables. The most important table was that of the King which was elevated on a low platform above the rest of the hall. Patti and Simon sat there beside Toria and Panri. Ezon and Meridia were there too. Many people commented on the great resemblance between the Royal children and Patti and Simon. Only that they were dressed differently it would have been impossible to tell them apart.

There was a court jester and he went from table to table telling jokes while the guests ate. Simon ate all he could; he was really hungry. Then there was a fanfare of trumpets, and the King made a speech. The whole hall fell silent and no one dared to eat a morsel of food during the speech, not even Simon.

When the banquet was over there was music and dancing. But Toria and Panri took Patti and Simon outside and they wandered around the corridors looking into stately rooms and running about playing. And Toria had a brilliant idea. They decided to change clothes for a while. When they returned

to the banquet-hall everybody bowed in front of Patti and
Simon, thinking they were the royal children. Toria and Panri
were tickled pink. But Ezon realized what was going on. He
took the children to one side and told them go outside again
and change clothes. Patti thought how splendid it had been
to be a Princess, even if only for a few minutes, but it was
not so nice for Ezon; he had to rebuke Toria and Panri.

The Prince and Princess accepted the reprimand good-
humouredly and when the evening's festivities were over they
escorted Patti and Simon to the main door of the Palace where
a carriage awaited to leave for Ezon's house, where a very
secret act was to be performed. As Toria and Panri watched
Patti and Simon leave with Ezon and Meridia, they felt certain
they would never again meet the two children who looked
so like them. But Meridia could have reassured them. She
had the power to ally to the stone in the shrine of Ezon's
father, and the stone pointed to other travels, other adventures
which would take Toria and Panri to Patti and Simon's world.
But that was in the future, and the future is always better
left unknown — until it happens.

When they got to Ezon's house they were taken straight
to the shrine. Meridia handed them the clothes they had worn
when they left Oakten and had fallen on to the deck of the
Atcheze. How she came to have them they had no idea, nor
did they ask. The shrine was gloomy and draped. Within a
circle was an altar on which had been placed a wand and a
ceremonial sword. There was also a cross made of roses, and
the emblems of the four elements; a cup for Water, a disc
for Earth, a dagger for Air, a wand for Fire. They could see
the Touchstone on the pillar outside the circle. They wanted
to go over and touch it, but Meridia said not to.

Then Ezon said good-bye. He shook their hands and smiled
sympathetically. But he did so from outside the circle. He
would not enter into it. Only then did Patti and Simon realize
that they were going home. They walked into the circle and

waved good-bye to Ezon. Meridia blindfolded them and placed the emblems in a circle around the altar. Then she led Patti and Simon three times around the inside of the circle. The stone and the rings on their fingers began to glow, and a whirl of light built up around them.

Meridia stepped from the circle and walked from the shrine. Ezon had already gone. He was waiting outside in the gardens where the sun was dipping from the sky in an orange ball of flame.

'Are they safe?' he asked Meridia.

'Yes, they have nothing to fear.' She touched Ezon gently on the shoulder. 'They will be back, but not for a very long time.'

In the shrine, in the circle, Patti and Simon slumped to the floor. The whirl of light continued to envelope their bodies until there was a blinding flash of light and the two children were gone. The stone, too, began to lose its glow. Almost instantly it faded and the shrine lay dark in the gloom of the twilight.

Ezon joked to Meridia.

'What?' she said.

'Some day I would like to take you on a holiday.'

'Where?'

'To a place called Oakten. Do you think that would be possible?'

'Everything is possible.'

And with that they sat in the garden and watched the last glow of the sun slip from the horizon.

Patti had a slight headache, and so had Simon. They were slumped over on the back seat of a car. It had crashed into a pole and there was broken glass everywhere. They sat up and looked out of the shattered side window. A crowd had gathered around the car, and an ambulance was speeding away from the crash scene.

Patti could see the man in the grey suit in the crowd. 'Simon, it's great! It's like we were never gone at all!'

Someone helped them from the car. The people in the crowd were slightly puzzled. They had not noticed the children when they had pulled Dresus from the wreck. Yet they must have been there — they had probably been thrown down between the seats when the car crashed.

A police-car pulled in, and two policemen jostled through the crowd.

'You okay?' they asked.

'Yes.'

'The driver, was he your father?'

'No. We got a lift from him, and he crashed.'

'A stranger?'

'Yes.'

'You shouldn't take lifts from strangers.'

'We won't. Never again.'

'That's good. Want a lift home?'

'No, we'll walk.'

'Say, you're those kids . . .'

'Yes, we're those kids!'

'Who was the driver, anyway?' queried one policeman of the crowd.

'The fellow that owns the car-lot. The one with all the holes in it.'

'Where's he from?'

'Nobody knows.'

'Well, I wish he'd go back to wherever it was.'

'Maybe he might.'

'Yes, maybe.'

'Was he badly hurt?'

'No, just seemed to be roarin' mad.'

Patti and Simon walked away from the crowd. The man in the grey suit followed them. They purposefully slowed down and allowed him to catch up.

'We know who you are,' said Patti defiantly.

'Who am I?'

'A spy! And you're not going to find out anything!'

'I'm wasting my time, then?'

'You bet you are!'

They walked on ahead of the man. Patti looked back, but the man was gone, probably to report to his superiors.

When they got to Patti's house Patti's mother asked Simon in for tea. 'You weren't gone long. What had you got in those packages?'

'Nothing much, Mum.'

'Your sister went out after you. She wants to bring you and Simon to a party.'

'When's the party, Mum?'

'Now!'

'Simon will have to go home and ask his parents.'

'Your sister has already seen them.'

'What's the party for, Mum?'

'It's a surprise for you and Simon.'

'Mum, we don't deserve it!'

'Of course you do. You are special.'

'But we're not special!'

'You are to me.'

Patti said no more. She and Simon went to the party. Patti's sister was already there, and rushed out to welcome them. There was no bickering or sulking. And when they were at the party a postman came around in a parcel-express-delivery van. He enquired for Patti and Simon and handed them a parcel each. When they opened the parcels they were amazed.

'What's yours?' asked Patti.

'A sword!'

'Mine's a crown!'

'Have a look at the date-mark on the parcels.'

But they could not make out the date or the place of posting. The post-marks were blurred.

They did not want the others to see the crown and sword, so they hid the parcels until the party was over and it was time to go home. Of course the crown and sword were the same as they had once found near the foot of the withered tree in the quarry; the same as Moorgate had placed in the tree at the castle garden.

When they got home they hid the crown and sword, and nobody, except Patti and Simon, was ever to see them again, and they never told anyone about their secret world, or the wonderful magical adventures that existed there.

And there were adventures, lots of adventures, and there continued to be adventures for longer than Gadua or anyone else would have time or patience enough to write down.

But as of that moment Patti and Simon went home. They were tired, and all they wanted to do was to go asleep. After all, it had been a very long, eventful day, longer than any of their friends, or parents, could possibly have imagined.

EPILOGUE

21. The Dream of Moorgate

A sleepy notion of squirrels occupied the fragile dreaminess of Moorgate's slumber. The squirrels had been on a picnic in a forest — not one of Atholle's island forests — but the forest Moorgate was born in. He even had notions of three of his brothers and four of his sisters chasing the squirrels away, the fine pin-lines of the squirrels' whiskers bold with brashness.

Once in the past, Moorgate had yearned for a home of his own. So, too, had his friends. Moorgate stirred in his sleep and sighed. He remembered his friends — there were nine of them — and they all had set out through the forest together, each in search of a separate home, but afraid to do so on their own. The kind of a home they wanted was a tree made from the changeling form of a human person. A human-changeling tree-home was far superior in warmth and comfort to ordinary tree-homes. And it was no problem for Moorgate or his fellow elves to conjure up a treasure and use it as bait to attract a victim. Absolutely no problem! All they needed were fools to fall for the trick.

Moorgate had nine trick treasures. His father had willed him four. His mother, two. His uncle, two. Yes, and he had found one himself. That made nine. A changeling-home was a must, especially since his parents had died, and there were too many at home, fighting and arguing over who owned the house.

Moorgate yawned, turned over, and dreamed on. He realized that he had made one costly mistake. He should never have set out in search of a tree-home with his friends. He should have gone on his own.

They had come to a clearing and Moorgate had conjured up a treasure. Ezon and Simon had come across it, only Ezon knew what it was and he threw a twig into the open treasure chest. A sapling sprung up in its place. The elves were furious when they saw what had happened. They felt cheated, and Moorgate was made to suffer. They handed him a brush and told him to brush the forest clear of leaves. An impossible task. Instead Moorgate had left the forest with Ezon and Simon. He never went back.

But he used up another treasure, eventually. The treasure that had trapped Dresus.

Moorgate turned over on his back. He lay awake. Someday he would go back home and visit his relatives and friends and make them apologize for having ordered him to sweep the forest clear of leaves. That, at least, would give him a sense of justice — even victory!

TOUCHSTONE

A mysterious crash-landing at the start of a
holiday – and Patti and Simon find themselves
in another worls. A world of flying horses,
dragons, wizards, elves, pirate captains.
A world in which the Kingdoms of the East
and the West are at war, and in which they
have a strange destiny to fulfill.
Uniting the two worlds is the touchstone ...
the magic emblem which binds reality to
fantasy, time present to time past, the light to
the half-light which dwells in the depths of
every imagination.
A marvellously vivid and dramatic novel
of the adventures of two earthlings
in another world.

*'Splendidly fast-paced and the descriptions
are memorable. Pamela Leonard's illustrations
add to the imaginative power of the novel.'*
JOHN LEDWIDGE, CLA OF IRELAND

*'A colourful and imaginative first novel –
eye-catching drawings by Pamela Leonard.'*
TOM CANTWELL, EVENING HERALD

ISBN 0 9 7962 52 2   £3 95

PETER REGAN is from Keadue in north Roscommon, but has lived in Bray, County Wicklow, all his life, where he now runs a small fuel and seed business.

Childhood holidays were spent in Roscommon, exploring the countryside (Turlough O Carolan, the last of the Irish bard-composers, is buried in nearby Kilronan cemetery), and imbibing a love of reading from his mother (history) and his grandmother (poetry and legend).

He was educated at St. Patrick's National School and Presentation College, Bray, and spent most of his spare time in the public library where he read 'everything'. He still remembers vividly books on Marco Polo, Stephen Foster and George Washington. In the adult field one of his great favourites is Steinbeck.

His main interest, apart from writing, is soccer. He used to organize schoolboy teams, and as 'Chick' Regan master-minded the Avon Glens and Brighton Celtic. Today he is a spectator, following the fortunes of Liverpool and Glasgow Celtic.

His first book was *Touchstone; Revenge of the Wizards* is the sequel.